SAILOR SOLDIER

Terrance Farrell

SAILOR SOLDIER

Before His Time

A Novel

Terrance Farrell

iUniverse, Inc.
New York Lincoln Shanghai

Sailor Soldier
Before His Time

iUniverse books may be ordered through booksellers or by contacting:

iUniverse
2021 Pine Lake Road, Suite 100
Lincoln, NE 68512
www.iuniverse.com
1-800-Authors (1-800-288-4677)

Because of the dynamic nature of the Internet, any Web addresses or links contained in this book may have changed since publication and may no longer be valid.

Certain characters in this work are historical figures, and certain events portrayed did take place. However, this is a work of fiction. All of the other characters, names, and events as well as all places, incidents, organizations, and dialogue in this novel are either the products of the author's imagination or are used fictitiously.

Maps and illustrations by Terrance Farrell.

ISBN: 978-0-595-45037-4 (pbk)
ISBN: 978-0-595-89349-2 (ebk)

Printed in the United States of America

For Marion

Maps
Approach to Boston Harbour 1812
Route taken to Niagara Penninsula Sept.–Oct. 1812
Queenston Heights October 13th 1812
Matthew's Journey Oct. 12–13 1812

CHAPTER 1

▼

The North Atlantic was a mad world of breaking waves, had been for several days, buffeting each vulnerable vessel that dared challenge the sea's massive power. Heavy layered clouds lay horizon to horizon, shuttering the sun, leaving only the occasional open slat through which the sun probed fingers of light that seemed to bend with the force of the wind. *HMCS Skeena*, a River-class Destroyer, steadfastly buried her eyes into each mountainous wave, only to rise, shake herself, and prepare to meet the next. Convoy SC42 consisted of sixty-six ships in nine columns that originally covered ten square miles of ocean. The convoy was rapidly losing formation and forward progress due to the force of the storm. The *Skeena* and its fellow escorts, the corvettes *Alberni, Orillia,* and *Kenogami*, had the responsibility to herd and protect, cowboys, if you will, but they also faced a visceral need. They were running low on fuel and needed to conserve. Naval headquarters determined that U-boats had formed an offensive line that stretched across SC42's planned course and the port director re-routed the convoy closer to the Greenland coast. An emergency transmission, the "dit-dit-dit" of the letter "s" in Morse code that signified a vessel under attack by submarine, was sent by a convoy straggler and received by *Skeena*. This confirmed that the main convoy would soon be discovered by the "wolf-pack." Radio silence was broken and a message that stated the facts, coded in naval cipher, was sent to the port director. Escort Group 24 needed help and it needed it now!

The final week of August and the first week of September, 1941, found the newly built *HMCS Blackfoot*, the Royal Canadian Navy's first Tribal-class Destroyer, cruising off the Nova Scotia coast. Commander Forron, Captain of

HMCS Blackfoot, referred to by the ship's company as "the Old Man," stared in seeming disbelief at the duty coder who had handed him the message. The Work-up Program, "WUPS," as the navy called it, of his destroyer had just been scrubbed. At 14:20 hours, September 8th, 1941, *HMCS Blackfoot* set course to intercept convoy SC42. For Yeoman of Signals Matthew Brock, mostly referred to as "Yeoman" or just "Yeo," although "Chief" was also correct, it was his first introduction to war. Huddled under his duffel coat with his binoculars protruding from under its hood, Matthew spotted a bright flash on the horizon that reflected off the clouds. It became a bright red glow, which grew, before fading to a flicker. Two flares soared skyward. *Blackfoot* had found the convoy. The Old Man ordered the ship's company to action stations.

"A message by megaphone, Sir. Submarine reported off the starboard bow of the merchant vessel bearing red three five," yelled Matthew, trying to make himself heard on the bridge from his station by the port twenty-four inch signal lamp.

"Port thirty," ordered the Old Man.

Blackfoot had been steaming in the opposite direction of the convoy, between rows seven and eight. Grey shapes of merchant vessels loomed out of the rain and spray. Now, in a delicate maneuver, *Blackfoot* was crossing the wake of a merchant vessel to intercept the U-boat. It was going to be tight. All eyes not otherwise employed were on the bow of the merchant vessel bearing down on their starboard side.

Flashes of bright yellow shattered the darkness, momentarily blinding Matthew. Yellow that was beautiful in contrast with the black of the sea, but whose source had the power to obliterate structure and end men's lives. The yellow radiated from its source, losing concentrated vigour and heat, cooling to a deep orange before being extinguished by the black of the sea. The flash was followed by sound, and its resonance was more horrifying. The ship split in half, spilling its cargo; machines of war, tanks, troop carriers, fighter planes in crates, are all consigned to the depths. Men, their sea-going apparel in flames, screaming, panic-driven and seeking relief, threw themselves into an extinguishing sea. The ship's lifeblood of thick bunker oil oozed over the sea's surface and calmed its turbulence. The oil sought the men that survived, covered them, and ignited. A survivor, shrouded by oil, reached out to Matthew, his eyes two white marbles in a black expanse of face, his contorted mouth perhaps emitting a sound that Matthew couldn't hear. Crimson flames caught up. The man who was perhaps a husband, maybe a father, most definitely a son, was for seconds, a burning pyre, before he disappeared beneath the oil calmed surface. The fire was extinguished after having snuffed a life, the man never to go home, as Matthew's father never came home, killed somewhere on the battlefields of Flanders.

It is impossible to observe a man's death with no ability to affect the circumstance. He gripped the railing that surrounded the signal platform and fought an internal battle for self, teeth clenched, shivering, bewildered, and mortified by what he had just seen.

Matthew was first to spot the submarine sitting beam-on and close, it's conning tower sticking up like an obscene thumb against the flaming ocean.

"Submarine! Dead ahead!" All personnel on *Blackfoot's* bridge peered forward, hoping to sort the U-boat from the wreckage of its victim. Matthew pointed it out to Lieutenant Cross, *Blackfoot's* Executive Officer, referred to as "Number One" by the Old Man, or "the Jimmy" by the ship's company. He pointed it out to the Old Man who quickly made a decision.

"Revolutions for twenty-five knots. Stand by to ram."

The port Oerlikon opened fire. Bright yellow sparks, like a hundred fireflies igniting their butt-ends, suddenly appeared on the U-boat's conning tower, marking bullet strikes. Through his binoculars, Matthew could see a man on the sub's conning tower who was bent over with his hands bracketing his mouth, shouting words that Matthew was unable to hear. All occupants of the conning tower disappeared from sight except for two, the man who yelled, and a man who appeared to be wounded. The man looked at *Blackfoot* bearing down on him, then at the wounded man who was reaching out to him, before descending into the conning tower, leaving the wounded man to drown. The face of the man reflected the U-boat's red-lit interior as he descended into the rapidly sinking tower. Matthew shivered, his hands clenched into fists, his jaw tightened, and his bowels turned liquid. He had just seen the face of the Devil reflecting the fires of Hell!

CHAPTER 2

▼

The higher submarine detection petty officer (HSD) called out the U-boat's range and bearing. "Stand-by to depth charge," said the Old Man, his voice sounding tightly controlled. The Oerlikon stopped firing. The Old Man seemed to acknowledge the silence with a quick glance toward the twin machine guns. "Inform *Skeena* of contact."

The anti-submarine control officer took command of the depth charge crews. "Set charges for ten fathoms. Fire by the recorder."

Matthew directed Signalman Macintyre, a "new-entry" who had joined *Blackfoot* right after graduation from signal school in St. Hyacinthe, Quebec, to raise the black submarine contact pennant. He took his pencil from his beard that, from habit, he used as a convenient place to keep it, and marked the time in his signal log. He was proud of each strand of grey hair that had a home in his auburn beard. There wasn't that many of them. To him, each one marked a life experience, much like the notches on a gun-fighter's pistol butt. There were a few grey hairs on his head, but he considered himself to be doing quite well for a man of thirty-six years.

Astern, the depth charges on the traps rolled into *Blackfoot's* wake, while the throwers deposited their charges out from each beam. It took only a minute before Matthew felt *Blackfoot* shake and saw the ocean boil. Towering waterspouts erupted close astern. He was mesmerized by the fountains of burning bunker oil mixed with white foam that fanned outward with such destructive beauty that he gave no thought to the U-boat's crew and the horror they may be experiencing. Judging from the grinding noise he heard emanating from *Blackfoot's* expansion joints as the destroyer vibrated, the depth charges were almost too close.

"Slow ahead," said the Old Man. The ASDIC was blinded for the moment by the turbulence of the depth charges. "If the target isn't destroyed, I'm betting that it turns to port to avoid the wreck." The bridge repeater suddenly started emitting the "ping-poink" of numerous contacts from irritating, frustrating clutter. "Multiple echoes," reported the HSD. The ASDIC was picking up the sinking freighter.

Black oily smoke enveloped *Blackfoot* in a noxious cloud. To breathe easier, Matthew pulled his duffel coat up to cover his mouth and nose. His eyes, however, began to water. With the surface cluttered with flotsam, flames, and oil, there was no way success could be confirmed by spotting any wreckage from the U-boat.

"Prepare to fire a second pattern. Set depth for ten fathoms," said the Old Man.

A second pattern of depth charges was dropped. With the greater depth settings it took longer for the eruptions. This time the huge columns of water lacked the same beauty as the first pattern. *Blackfoot* shook but not as violently. There was only the increased motion from the stormy sea that was no longer tamed by bunker oil. *Blackfoot* had cleared the wreckage area. All hands astern kept their eyes peeled for a fresh oil slick, perhaps wreckage, any sign that they'd destroyed the U-boat.

Blackfoot continued with a square search for thirty minutes but was unable to regain contact with the U-boat. The Old Man broke off the search and steamed to the escort screen position assigned to *Blackfoot* by *Skeena*. From his position as yeoman it was Matthew's responsibility to keep the Old Man informed on happenings with the convoy and its escorts. Convoy SC42 was taking a terrible beating. During the evening of September 9th, the steamer *Numeric* had the bottom blown out of her, followed later by the steamer *Empire Springbuck*. Throughout the night the convoy also lost the steamers *Baron Pentland, Winterswijk, Stargaard, Sally Maersk,* and the "Cam" ship *Empire Hudson*. With the approach of daylight the wolf-pack appeared to pull back and discontinue action. This allowed Matthew to catch a little "kip." By noon the next day, the convoy's protection was bolstered by the addition of the corvettes *Moose Jaw* and *Chambly*, fresh from Halifax. Just after their arrival, a U-boat torpedoed the steamer *Thistleglen*, and immediately came under attack by three escorts. This action brought Matthew back to the bridge feeling quite rumpled, having slept "all standing," hungrily chewing a leftover bully-beef sandwich. He spent a busy afternoon and the dog watches repeating signals to the convoy from the convoy commodore, as well as handling messages to *Blackfoot* from other escorts and the senior officer escorts (SOE). By four bells of the evening watch he was too hungry to complain when handed a mug of kye along with another bully-beef sandwich. This one was slightly fresher than the one he ate earlier.

The Jimmy bent to a voice pipe and listened. His face became animated and his voice betrayed his excitement when he reported to the Old Man.

"Radar contact bearing three two four degrees at a range of three five zero zero yards … possible submarine."

The Old Man leapt from his chair. "Steer three two four degrees, revolutions for twenty-five knots. Illuminate the target!" The illumination officer spoke into his telephone.

Macintyre was already bending the submarine contact pennant to the halyard closest to the mast. From aft came a loud bang as X-mount fired off starshells. Under Matthew's feet, *Blackfoot* vibrated as she worked up to speed.

She heeled to come on course. The wind swept sea sprayed the foredeck. Matthew searched the gloom waiting for the starshells to burst. When they did, they were man made suns that slowly parachuted toward the ocean's surface. Their light reflected from the cloud cover and a churning fog bank that lay to starboard. The reflections gave them added intensity, highlighting the low profile of a U-boat that was beam to the sea and rolling violently. For some reason, he had a warm feeling deep within his gut that told him that it was the same U-boat. This puzzled him.

"A and B guns, commence, commence!" yelled the gunnery officer, known to both captain and crew as "Guns." Both forward turrets fired simultaneously. Matthew plugged his ears with his fingers, not having time to use the cotton wads he kept in his pocket. He opened his mouth to relieve any pressure caused by the concussion of the guns firing. However, he failed to look away to protect his sight and he was blinded by the muzzle flashes. Looking away was an action needed because the fossil equivalents in the navy's top brass didn't see the need for flash-less powder. Hell, the Royal Navy had it, and if you want to talk about fossils. He also had to contend with the smoke and his eyes were awash with tears. When his vision cleared so that he could see adequately, although his ears still rang, the target was emerging from towering columns of water marking near misses. The U-boat foreshortened as it turned toward *Blackfoot*, quickly becoming a small target. It was bow down and submerging.

"Inform HSD of target's range and bearing! Send contact report to *Skeena*! Stand by depth charges!" It sounded like the Old Man was becoming a seasoned veteran.

"Torpedoes ... dead ahead and closing!" The starboard lookout was already starting to recoil and to anxiously look around as if searching for a safe place to hide. His face was a mask of fear that contrasted the calm feeling he projected to Matthew who was standing near him. This puzzled Matthew because he was also felt calm, comfortable in fact, although his survival wasn't certain. He barely heard the Old Man's helm order and the acknowledgment of depth charge readiness because he started to focus inward; composed by the knowledge that death is the most natural thing in the world. He noticed, but failed to register, that his hands were surrounded by a radiating blue light that softly pulsed. The whirring, vibrating turbines, the hiss and crash of wave and spatter of spray, the creaks and groans of a speeding destroyer, took on the monastic hum of a single musical note. He stared blankly at the on-coming trails of disturbed water that began from a single point and separated as they approached. He was no longer conscious of thought.

CHAPTER 3
▼

The hardest target for a submarine is a vessel that is bow-on. Each torpedo passed on opposite beams, so the expected meeting of destroyer and torpedo didn't occur. All on-deck personnel who'd stood motionless for the past forty-five seconds resumed activity; the whole experience was like a stoppage in time. Matthew let out a sigh and shook his arms to get rid of the pins and needles he felt there. He slowly turned his hands as he inspected them before bringing them to his face and rubbing them down his beard, knocking out the pencil he kept there. He absently watched its flight as it bounced off the screen before falling overboard. It slowly turned end for end before being lost in the bow wave.

"What the hell happened?" Matthew spoke out loud as he again studied his hands.

Macintyre looked confused. "Two torpedoes just missed us, Yeo!"

"Yes, I know ... but—" He shut his mouth and turned so that Macintyre wouldn't see his face. He looked to starboard where he saw a rolling fog bank moving towards *Blackfoot*. HSD reported on the U-boat's position.

"Echo bearing three one five degrees, range twelve hundred yards, classified submarine. Doppler indicating range to target decreasing."

"Very good. Port ten. Stand-by depth charges. Helm amidships."

As the flares died a sizzling death, the "ping-poing" of the ASDIC bridge repeater reached into the darkness. The sound reflected off the fog bank, bringing Matthew's concentration back to its looming presence. In all his years growing up on the west coast, and all his years at sea, he had never seen a fog bank like it. It was approaching *Blackfoot* as surf does a holiday beach, only this image was menacing—like a shark in the surf. To port, and to starboard, long fingers of fog were reaching out to *Blackfoot,* to encircle her with a mothering protection, or perhaps a mother's suffocation. He noted a difference in colour. The usual white mistiness of a fog bank was replaced by a murky mauve, which shifted to a cold shade of blue-green. This fog had meanness to it, an advancing wall that took on the form of a dark scowling face, which, when Matthew looked at it, he was instantly captivated, unable to look away, unable to speak. On and on it came, its dark brow turning in on itself again and again, while its two appendages continued to encircle *Blackfoot.*

The activities on the bridge where the tracking of the submarine continued— the HSD reported an instant echo—fell on deaf ears. His conscious mind was overwhelmed by the sound of the forbidding voice of the malevolent face. It was the voice of a million men contained within the voice of one man who was laughing with the joy of all mankind. It was as if a million tongues were screaming the anger of all man's ages. It was the cries of a billion loved ones lamenting the dear departed of all man's wars. It combined the voices of a million men from a thousand different eras to speak as one terrible voice about the nature of man in common bond with warfare.

Within the labyrinth of Matthew's soul the demon that dwells there awakened and rejoiced to an understanding of the harangue. For a few seconds, Matthew was cognizant of an incredible knowledge, a comprehension of natural truths that are reserved primarily for seers and saints. It was an instructive understanding that expanded the boundaries of ordinary existence that would enable him to reach for the chalice of life's outer limits. It was a communication between two entities that started long ago and would never end.

The destroyer was rolled to beam's-end and back by a sudden violent up-welling that belched spheres of thick, choking fog. Hungry whirlpools that swallowed whatever came near seemingly beckoned to *Blackfoot,* daring her to come close enough for them to grab. *Blackfoot* steered clear by dodging to port or to starboard, not guided by man, but by some unseen but powerful hand. She swerved to starboard to miss a particularly large whirlpool, but was caught by one that opened right in her path. She was grabbed by its vortex where its powerful suction pulled her under. The communication was severed, the knowledge withdrew, and the demon resumed its sleep in the comfort of Matthew's soul.

It started slowly at first, individual pictures that originated in his mind's eye were projected onto a wall of grey water that moved horizontally at high speed. It was only a fleeting glimpse, but he recognized the red brick school he'd attended, just up from Beach Avenue in Vancouver. The picture was replaced by an image of his younger self. Picture replaced picture, each faster than the one before, until there was no separation. Matthew was watching a motion picture of his own making. This should have had a profound effect on Matthew, but he felt detached, as if he was just part of the audience, and that he wasn't really that boy sitting at a school desk flipping through a book. His viewpoint was looking over the shoulder of his younger self where he could see the book and what was on the page. The boy that was Matthew stopped turning pages at one that was familiar. There, at the top of the page, was an engraving of a soldier who stood ram-rod stiff, looking to his left in profile. His left hand rested on the hilt of his sword, and his right hand pointed to a scroll on a writing table. This portrait of Matthew's famous ancestral uncle, Major General Sir Isaac Brock, hero of the War of 1812, and a source of pride in the Brock family name ever since, was forever engraved in Matthew's mind.

The image vanished as the wall of water fell away. Matthew stretched and yawned, while a relaxation flowed into his limbs, taking away an ache in his hands. He stood still a moment to get his bearings, the sounds of a living and working destroyer slowly invaded his consciousness. What he was seeing started to dawn on him. Night had suddenly become day. The ocean had only a light chop. The sky was blue with only a few puffy cumulus clouds on the horizon to starboard. The dark shadow of a racing destroyer played the tops of the waves off the port bow. The sun was hot on the back of his parka hood.

A multitude of questions tumbled through his mind. He concentrated on trying to sort them out, but the rail in front of him caught his attention. It was twisted in two places. He slowly reached out and tentatively took hold of the bends, already sensing what he would find, and was afraid. The mutations fit his hands perfectly.

CHAPTER 4

▼

A bright sun warmed the decks of *HMCS Blackfoot* as she sped through a light chop at twenty knots. The horizon, through all points of the compass, was empty of merchant steamers and their guardian naval vessels. The Old Man, who had shed his heavy duffel coat, was manning the voice pipes himself, talking to HSD, radar, TS, HF/DF, and plot, trying to establish contact with, or determine the whereabouts of, Convoy SC42. He had the TS break radio silence to attempt making contact with *Skeena* or port director.

Matthew, now on the bridge, could only stand and observe as the Jimmy, Guns, action officer of the watch, navigation officer and gunner (T) stood in a group muttering amongst themselves, leaving him out of hearing range. The Jimmy left the group and walked to where he'd left his duffel coat and pulled his pipe from the left pocket. He walked to the binnacle and stared at the compass before re-joining the group. Guns searched his pockets and handed the Jimmy a match.

The Old Man sat heavily in his captain's chair and called the Jimmy over. Matthew was now close enough to hear their discussion. He listened with great interest, though he pretended not to listen, if that's possible in the close confines of a destroyer's bridge.

"What do you make of this, Number One?" said the Old Man.

"I think,"—the Jimmy paused to remove the pipe from his mouth—"I think it must have something to do with that fog bank. However, I don't know how long we were in the fog, but by my watch it was twenty-one thirty-seven hours when we entered the fog and my watch now reads, let's see … ten fourteen hours, so …" He shrugged. "I do know that we are on the same course that we were on before we entered the fog bank."

"Are you telling me that we spent twelve hours in the fog? That we have lost twelve hours?"

"No, sir!" said the Jimmy who took a suck on his pipe and didn't seem to care where the smoke went. "Not necessarily. Would you excuse me for a moment, sir?" The Jimmy moved to the voice pipes. "Bridge … Engine room." He listened. "How long since you got your last order, Chief?" He nodded. "I see!" The Jimmy faced the Old Man. "He received his last order only twenty minutes ago … if that makes sense."

"But I haven't ordered a change of revolutions or compass heading since we left the fog!" The Old Man was sounding frustrated. The Jimmy must have felt Matthew's eyes on him and suddenly realized that he was listening to their conversation. The Jimmy turned to look at him.

"What do you make of it, Yeo?" The Jimmy's question startled Matthew.

Matthew didn't really have an answer, but then again, he didn't want to admit that. How would he explain feeling like he'd just awakened from a satisfying sleep when they came out of the fog bank, or the fact that the bends in the signal platform rail were made by his hands, when he couldn't explain it to himself? He looked at the expectant face of the Jimmy and then the stoic visage of the Old Man. He had to say something—hopefully intelligent!

"Go ahead, Yeo," said the Jimmy. Matthew relaxed.

"The chief engineer wasn't on deck, sir. Only personnel on deck would have noticed the fog. If things are as they appear, we may have lost twelve hours. If we have, then it only took minutes to lose them." The Jimmy nodded and the Old Man looked directly at him. "If I may continue, sir, if we did lose twelve hours, on this course, and with this speed, we shouldn't be standing here in warm sunshine. We'd more likely be fending off fugging icebergs."

"Damn it! You're right. Good thinking, Yeo! Anything else you can add … and don't use that "F" word. That word and the word it's derived from are not allowed. You know that."

"Sorry, sir." Matthew took a deep breath to relax. "We can only guess at the time of day, and for that matter, we can only guess at the date." The Old Man was staring at him. "We don't know where the convoy is or where the U-boat is." He swallowed, knowing that he was about to stick his neck out much like a turkey at Christmas—under the blade of an axe. Only difference here was that he knew who held the axe. "With respect, sir, I believe we are lost!"

The Old Man snorted and glared from Matthew to the Jimmy.

"Yes ... ah ..." The Jimmy addressed the Old Man. "If you will excuse me, sir, I believe we should include the navigation officer in our discussion."

Matthew moved away as he was now officially out of the discussion and glad of it. He needed a drink!

The next fifteen minutes was busy for the navigation officer. He used his sextant to bring the sun to the horizon, noted the time and disappeared to the plot room which was located immediately under the bridge. When he reappeared, he approached the Old Man to make his report. Matthew was still within earshot.

"Sir, about our position ..." The navigation officer paused and looked at the Jimmy, then back to the Old Man. Even Matthew could hear him swallow. "I have absolutely no idea where we are. If the date is September eleventh, and that is what I've assumed ..." He took a deep breath. "My intercept places us over fifteen hundred miles toward the sun from our last plotted position. I would suggest that we wait until I can take a noon shot. It will give us our correct position."

The Old Man showed no reaction but sat quietly for a minute or two, glaring at the sweating navigation officer. He stood up and paced to each wing of the bridge and stared at the respective horizons. He turned, gave a slight nod to the navigation officer, and walked to the public address system.

The system snapped the air with electrical pops and crackles. "Attention ship's company. This is your captain. Although there are some of you, those working below decks that have not noticed anything different ... it seems we've lost contact with the convoy and from what I can determine, apparently we've somehow lost twelve hours. I will keep you informed as things develop. Carry on." The system popped when he shut it off.

From somewhere along the weather deck came the yell, "The Old Man's bonkers!"

With the noon sight, the navigation officer was able to plot *Blackfoot's* position as approximately five hundred and thirty miles north of Bermuda. The Old Man altered course for Halifax. *Blackfoot* steamed toward the horizon at a slow but steady ten knots to conserve fuel, drawing air through her ventilators, the hum of her turbines giving a feeling of reassurance as ship's routine carried on through the afternoon and both dog watches.

Matthew spent the evening watch in the chiefs and petty officers mess where a group was gathered around the heavy mess table discussing the day's events. Having no answers, he only listened to what was being said. He thought a couple of times that he should say something but then thought better of it. He turned in at six bells, this time undressing to his pusser underwear, but leaving his outer clothing and sea boots where he could grab them quickly if needed.

The eastern horizon slowly brightened as the upper limb of the sun rose from the sea to a clear sky. When Matthew came on watch and logged in, the sun was a warm globe well above the horizon. As he expected, the ocean was empty of other traffic, *Blackfoot* seemed to be the only vessel floating. He climbed down to the port signal platform and said good morning to Macintyre, who was the duty signalman. He yawned and scratched himself, suffering from crotch-rot and badly in need of a shower. There was absolutely nothing to do. He went through the previous days events in his mind as he stared vacantly at the horizon. He saw it three times before it registered. There was something out there, something white, he could only see it when *Blackfoot* rose on a swell, but he was definite. He climbed the ladder to the bridge and approached the officer of the watch.

"Sir!" He got the man's attention. "There is an unidentified object just over the horizon bearing approximately red four five." The OOW looked shocked.

"Oh! Very good, Yeo!" The OOW reported to the Old Man who stood up from his captain's chair, grabbed a pair of binoculars, and crossed to the port side. He began scanning the horizon. Matthew returned to the port signal platform where Macintyre was also staring at the horizon.

"Could be a vessel in distress," said Matthew. "It looks like smoke, although it doesn't appear to have the black, oily quality of a ship on fire."

"Action stations," ordered the Old Man. *Blackfoot* altered course. Never in a thousand years would Matthew expect what rose above the horizon that day. He noticed his hands. He was hanging onto the bends in the rail which he'd made with his own hands.

He jerked his hands away. They felt burnt!

Chapter 5

▼

"What do you make of it, Number One?" asked the Old Man in a matter-of-fact tone.

"Well, sir, there appears to be masts."

"Does there appear to be sails on them?"

"Yes, sir, I would confirm that ... although I would hesitate to do so."

The Old Man remained silent.

As *Blackfoot* fast approached, the masts rose over the horizon to reveal two old fashioned sailing vessels, floating side to side in apparent conflict, made evident by the flame and smoke erupting from between them. Noise reached *Blackfoot* as rolling thunder.

Matthew returned to the bridge to get a better view. The scene that was unfolding in front of him was uncanny. A scene that was difficult for him to grasp. Perhaps it was a spectre from the past. Maybe it's a movie being filmed, an Errol Flynn movie. He was rooted to his spot, sorting his mind to get his thoughts in order. What the hell is happening to him? He shouldn't see the things he's seeing, or feel the way he feels. But then, the Old Man sees what he sees, and so does the Jimmy. Maybe he's not going crazy! Maybe we are all fugging bonkers!

The Old Man broke his silence. "Tell me, Number One, if I am correct in my observation. Would you say one of those vessels is flying the White Ensign?"

"Yes, sir, I can confirm that. The other appears to be flying an older style American ensign."

To Matthew both officers sounded calm, almost surreal. The navy must have changed them into unfeeling instruments of pusser certitude. One of them could just swear or something.

"I have to accept the reality that they're there, no matter how badly I may want to discount it! Now the question is what the hell do I do about it?"

The Jimmy remained silent.

"Have Guns prepare to open fire, Number One." The Old Man sounded mechanical.

Matthew suddenly felt chilled. He stared at the Old Man, not bothering to hide the fact he was listening.

"But, sir, I …"

"Don't but me, Number One! What I see out there is a ship flying the same ensign as us, engaged in mortal conflict with a ship flying the ensign of a foreign power. It is my determination that we should render assistance to our ensign, no matter what manner of vessel is flying it. I don't know why I have to explain this to you!"

"But, sir, the foreign flag is American. They aren't at war with us. They're neutrals. Shouldn't we investigate first? It may be just a pretend fight. They may be shooting blanks. There must be an answer to this. There has to be some reasonable explanation! A wooden ship like that … hell … it wouldn't have a chance against us." The Jimmy took a deep breath. "It would be murder, sir, murder of sailors who are our friends!"

Matthew's respect for the Jimmy increased. The Jimmy will have to tear his certificate in pusser passiveness off the wall and pin up one that says "human." He also may as well tear up his commission.

The Old Man spoke angrily. "Just do as you're told!"

The Jimmy relented. "Aye-aye, sir." He nodded to the gunnery officer. "Guns, prepare to fire."

"And, Number One, fire only A-mount, and aim to just miss the target vessel."

"Aye-aye, sir." The Jimmy sounded relieved.

After firing, *Blackfoot* increased speed to thirty knots. The shells exploded close alongside the sailing vessel flying the American ensign, cascading large volumes of water across her deck. The fight went out of the contending vessels and the firing slackened, both ships rocked in the swell. The smoke that had welled up between them slowly drifted downwind. *Blackfoot* approached to pass the starboard bow of the American vessel. The Old Man ordered a twenty-degree turn to starboard and she passed the port side of the sailing vessel at high speed. The

American vessel rocked in *Blackfoot's* swell. Tattered sails slapped against the vessel's masts. Broken rigging swung and yards swayed. All the while *Blackfoot's* four turrets rotated to keep her guns trained on the American vessel.

As *Blackfoot* turned to port to pass astern of the sailing vessel, Matthew was able to pick out the name carved into her stern. Her name was *Chesapeake*.

"Chesapeake. Where have I heard that name?"

"You said something, Yeo?" It was the Jimmy.

"Oh, I'm sorry, sir! I didn't realize that I'd spoken out loud."

"You've heard that name before?"

"Yes, sir, somewhere, although I can't think of where at this moment. I do recognize the type of vessel, sir." Matthew's thoughts started to tumble. There he goes, sticking his neck out again. Never volunteer. Speak only when spoken to. He kept forgetting that. "She is a frigate of the type used by the Royal Navy in Nelson's time."

"We both know that's impossible," said the Jimmy. "Wooden frigates don't exist nowadays except where they are preserved as a museum."

Matthew pointed. "Look at the uniforms worn by those men at her aft rail. They are the style worn in Nelson's time. That's also impossible!"

The Jimmy said nothing.

The ship's boats were trailing by a line behind the *Chesapeake*. Chickens stood on the cowlings and flapped their wings to keep their balance. One boat, with a goat in it, almost capsized when the goat panicked as *Blackfoot* passed.

Matthew was able to study each vessel as *Blackfoot* bore down on the one flying the White Ensign. He presumed that the ship was British. Both ships were painted in the same pattern. Each had a black hull with a yellow stripe lengthwise on the level of their gun ports. Both showed scars from the battle *Blackfoot* had interrupted. There were jagged holes in their hulls, tattered sails hung from their yards, and shrouds were cut to ribbons. Irish pennants could be observed in the rigging where lines had been sliced.

A longboat below the entry port of the vessel was being manned. From the entry port emerged a man uniformed in the style of the early Royal Navy. He was wearing a sword.

Blackfoot passed astern of this vessel as well. Across her stern, ornately carved and covered with gold leaf, was her name. Matthew's hands felt hot. The vessel's name was *Shannon*.

Matthew would sooner face a U-boat any day than lead a boarding party toward an unknown quarry. He shouldn't be there. This needed the authority of an officer. The bulwark of *Shannon* was lined with sailors, standing quietly, watching his approach. From somewhere deep within the vessel came ghoulish, blood-curdling screams. Matthew's mind went into full gear. Jesus! It had to be wounded men undergoing the knife and saw of some primitive surgeon. Shit! Those men along the bulwarks, they are aiming rifles at us! No! Those are muskets! They couldn't be! Of course not!

A tall, thin man, with epaulettes on each shoulder, was standing at the rail near the stern. He had a speaking trumpet in his hand. Matthew guessed he must be the captain and that he was about to speak.

"Avast there! Identify yourself and your business."

Matthew stood up, balancing himself in the rocking whaler, while those manning the oars backed water. In his mind he had many questions. How should he handle this? Fug, he had no idea! He used to know, but that was ages ago. He learned it in a training course somewhere. He drew his pistol and sat down. He had to think. The pistol! It felt warm. He looked astern at the bridge of *Blackfoot*. It seemed to him that the whole ship's company was watching him. Shit! The pistol was getting bloody hot! He put it back into its holster. He wondered why he drew it in the first place. He decided to go for it and stood up.

"I am Yeoman Matthew Brock of His Majesty's Canadian Ship *Blackfoot*. I'm coming aboard." He sat down. "All away together."

White smoke erupted from the muskets of the men that lined the bulwarks. Musket balls ripped the air around him. The ocean around the whaler erupted in miniature geysers. Holy shit! They fired on him! It can't be! Those aren't real ships. They are only pretend ships, fighting a pretend war. Yet, they tried to kill him and his men. Holy shit! They wanted to kill us!

The whole side of *Shannon* exploded in smoke and fire, followed by the hellish scream and concussion of passing cannon balls. The whaler came close to capsizing from the startled reaction of Matthew and his crew. They all ducked for non-existent cover. Astern, *Blackfoot* rang from the impact of the cannon balls.

Matthew realized that those assholes were actually looking for a fight. *Blackfoot* answered with one twin 20mm Oerlikon, its bullets snapped over Matthew and his men, and smashed through the wooden bulwarks and exploded the men behind them into unrecognizable human fragments. It fired for all of fifteen seconds. There was no more hostile action by *Shannon*. Matthew's initial thought was that they asked for a fight and, by God, they got it. Good for Blackfoot! Realization set in. My God! Good for Blackfoot? There are dead men over there!

Matthew waited, dripping with sweat. He wanted to vomit at what he'd just seen. He swallowed. He swallowed again. He needed to visit the head, badly.

The *Shannon's* captain raised his speaking trumpet. "Permission to board granted."

CHAPTER 6

▼

His feet were sodden, leaving puddles on the deck. He should have waited for the *Shannon's* hull to roll away from him, thus lifting him away from the water after he leapt to the tumble home ladder. He was able to maintain his footing on the small steps by utilizing the two manropes that were thrown to him from the entry port. He straightened his jacket and manoeuvred his ass to get his shorts loosened in his crotch. He stood facing a young lad wearing a short blue tunic with white tabs on his stiff collar. At his cuffs were three brass buttons. He couldn't be a chief petty officer. He was too damn young. The term "snotty" came to mind. Matthew remembered the history of the three brass buttons he wore on his own sleeve. During Nelson's time, midshipmen, boys in their mid to late teens, wore three brass buttons sewn onto their cuffs to prevent them from wiping their nose on their sleeve, hence the name "snotty." But that was impossible! In front of him lay the mangled, grotesque dead. They weren't pretending! They were dead! They were killed by the Old Man's order. Matthew swallowed hard.

"Accompany me, if you please, sir," said the young lad.

Matthew noted that his cox'n had come on deck. He carried a Sten gun cradled in his arms. Matthew indicated that the cox'n should remain at the entry port before he followed the boy along the wooden deck that was covered in sand. He watched where he stepped, avoiding puddles of red and ribbons of red. The blood of the dead! He stepped past the dead; stepped over the dead; surprised he was able to do so without gagging. He passed what appeared to be ancient cannon; passed dirty, smelly men, with cloths in bad need of repair; their faces weather beaten, leather-like, with numerous blackheads. Their teeth, if they had any, were in a bad state. Their bare feet were callused and filthy. Their badly callused hands were black as tar. Each man had a tarred pigtail. What affected Matthew the most was that their eyes were dull, as if devoid of life.

The lad led him aft past a large double helm to where the man Matthew presumed was the captain was busy writing on a slate with chalk. The lad stood quietly. So did Matthew.

He took the opportunity to look around, still not willing to believe. He had walked the deck of a frigate once before. The *USS Constitution*, commonly known as "Old Ironsides," was the principal frigate for America's naval effort in the war of 1812. He was able to tour the *Constitution* when his ship was on a courtesy visit to Boston in 1938. This vessel was almost a mirror image. Cannon were positioned along the deck as far as the entry port where the cox'n stood. Amidships, along both port and starboard sides, were gangways. The middle section of the deck was not planked in. There were large beams spanning the gap from gangway to gangway. More cannon could be seen on the forecastle.

The captain looked up and, with his hand, dismissed the boy before meeting Matthew's eyes. He was a man of obvious authority, and judging by his red hair, what Matthew could see of his side burns and hair that protruded from under his ridiculous hat, he probably had a temper. The man had full cheeks, a slightly hooked nose, and the beginnings of a double chin. Fug! It must be a movie set. The man is wearing a costume for a uniform.

"Identify yourself, sir, and what manner of ship is yours?" The captain's breath was foul.

"I am Yeoman Brock of His Majesty's Canadian Ship—"

"Canadian! Do you take me for an idiot, sir?" The captain's neck was turning red, showing his anger.

"No, sir, *Blackfoot* is a Canadian ship—"

"From where?"

"From Halifax, sir. We left there not more than two weeks ago to—"

"You presume on my intelligence, sir!" The captain was now very angry. "I was in Halifax not two weeks past. I petition your word and trust in your truth as to manner of vessel and like of person. Your vessel yonder … is she one of Robert Fulton's inventions?"

Matthew suddenly shivered. Pins and needles of fear climbed his legs. Robert Fulton? Shit! Where has this guy been?

"No, sir, she is of British design …" Hell! He'd better cut to the quick on this. However, he must do it tactfully. "Sir, I haven't had the pleasure of being introduced, and may I inquire as to this vessel?"

"Broke is my name, Post Captain. This vessel, entrusted to my hand by the Lord of the Admiralty is His Britannic Majesty's Ship *Shannon*!"

He seemed to be calming down. Matthew noted the man's eyes were searching his uniform which had red Canada badges and red trade badges. There were three brass buttons on each cuff that indicated his rank was chief petty officer-second class.

"Your uniform is not familiar, and of your vessel I do not know. Your shoulders proclaim Canada, but this cannot be so. I know of no naval force of Canada but that subject to His Majesty. A snotty you are, but who, prey tell, are you?"

A snotty? Oh yeah, his three brass buttons. He thinks that Matthew is a midshipman!

He tried to keep his voice from quivering. "With respect, sir, I'm not ..." To hell with it! "It is my captain who wishes to know just who, and what, you are."

"Your captain is presumptuous, sir!" The captain was angry again, his voice becoming hard. "Who I am is no secret! Of your captain, he should be here in your stead! By what rank is he addressed?"

"He is addressed as the captain, sir! He has the rank of commander. Commander Forron."

"Commander! Then he should attend to me!" His voice became very hard. "As senior naval officer present, I expect, at your captain's peril to do or say otherwise, his respect and the truth of what my eyes behold. Good day to you, sir!" The captain turned his back to Matthew.

"Sir?" The captain kept his back turned. Matthew felt his anger rising. Just who the hell does he think he is? Obviously he's a cock-sure, proud son-of-a-bitch. Proud enough to get his men killed! "Sir?" The captain turned and glared, his face crimson with anger, his mouth open as if to speak. Matthew didn't let him. He stood his ground.

"Sir, your costume is naval, quite grand in fact, albeit a little ancient, as is this ship. To say that my captain must pay you respect as a senior officer is absurd, to say the least. Commander Forron is the only naval officer anywhere near here and demands your respect and explanation as to your presence, that of your vessel, and the other off to starboard."

"I ... I have had enough of your insubordination, sir!" The captain was so angry that he splattered saliva when he spoke. "Lieutenant Davis. Have this ... this man"—he took a deep breath—"removed from my presence and my vessel."

Matthew turned and beckoned to the cox'n who approached at the double. "This person obviously didn't learn anything from the demonstration of *Black-*

foot's firepower, so perhaps a demonstration of personal firepower is in order." He spoke loud enough for the captain and those near him to hear.

The cox'n cocked his Sten gun, tucked the wire butt under his right arm, his left arm went under the magazine to grip the barrel. He pointed it at the mizzen-mast and let off a short burst, scarring the mast, the bullets sending chips of wood flying. Matthew didn't take his eyes off the captain, whose face remained angry and determined, but his eyes betrayed a fear. Matthew told the cox'n to keep his eyes open for any funny business and then addressed the captain.

"I would suggest, sir, that my questions be answered in a polite and proper manner!" There was still fear there, quite visible in fact. His answer, however, showed a pride perhaps only found in a person of considerable authority.

"As a warship, *Shannon* requires no evidence, her record in service exemplary. As to your vessel, a warship I cannot deny. To do so would be to forsake my own eyes. Weight in arms I relinquish to your captain, for his demonstration, and yours just now are persuasive. However, as to your credentials, I am not convinced. A naval officer you are not for your manner and uniform are derogatory. Your shoulders announce Canada, a colony of which I have visited and know well of hand that it has no naval authority. As senior naval officer present, the American captain notwithstanding, I demand due homage from your commander!"

Matthew showed his frustration.

"Sir ... you are but a dressed up actor and your vessel is nothing but a set. Actors do not demand the respect of naval officers. I—"

"You think me a charlatan, sir?" yelled the captain, clenching his fists. "And the deck upon which you stand naught but a stage constructed of paste board and sacking? You insult me, sir, and through me, His Majesty. I'm of half a mind to call you out, career be damned!" He paused before continuing, seeming to consider something. He glanced at the Sten gun the cox'n held, and then across the water at *Blackfoot*. When he spoke again, his voice had mellowed a bit.

"However, caution is prudent 'cept to say that thorough of thought and judicious of tongue, you are not. Be particular lest you commit grievous offence. I say, as senior naval officer present, that you will offer proper respect forthwith or this discourse is ended for cumbersome it proves."

Still stubborn, the bastard! Well, Matthew could be stubborn as well and he wasn't going to back down. This required courage.

"Nothing is ended until I say so, sir. As you say, you relinquish to *Blackfoot* force of arms. Forget that at your peril. What you did by firing upon *Blackfoot* is commit an act of piracy. Cover this man, cox'n. As the senior of two, and only two, naval representatives present, I am placing you and this vessel under arrest. You will accompany me to *Blackfoot*."

"Sir." It was the snotty. "A dispatch, sir." The boy handed a slip of paper to the captain, then turned and fled.

The captain glanced at it before holding it out for Matthew to take. "It is for you."

"Oh! Thank you. It's from my captain." He took the note and what it said sent a pencil point of cold fear down the length of his spine. He looked at the captain who was regarding him intently. Shit! All that happened over the past two days could, perhaps, be explained. Now he had to manage what was asked of him. This was going to require some tact.

"Your countenance, if I may be so bold, is growing pale. I pray the news is not tragic." The captain sounded concerned.

Matthew looked from the note to the captain, back to the note, then back to the captain. He wished he had more time. He had to think. He'd just threatened the man with arrest. Shit! If this proved true, he was in for it—big time!

"You may think this petty, sir, but"—he took a deep breath—"my captain wishes that you confirm today's date."

"With certainty." The captain gave a snort, probably signifying contempt for the question. "With God's blessing, this day is the twelfth of September."

Matthew felt some tension drain away, but he had a second question. The tension returned. This would show him to be an idiot.

"What year?"

The captain raised his eyebrows; perhaps at the tentative quality Matthew could hear in his own voice, perhaps sensing a change in Matthew's attitude.

"It is the year of our Lord ... eighteen twelve!"

C H A P T E R   7

▼

Matthew sat in silence, looking toward the English Captain. Shit! What he'd found out still had to be proved. He knew it was the Old Man's intention to find the truth, for he'd entrusted him with the task. The meeting was taking place in the cabin of the English Captain. It was bright compared to the deck forward of the cabin's bulkhead, what the English Captain described as the gun deck. Windows spanned the stern bulkhead, the thick glass distorting the outside view. An un-upholstered window seat spanned the rear of the cabin. Several potted plants were arranged along the seat. The deck was spread with a canvas that was painted in black and white squares. There were cabins port and starboard, probably the captain's galley, sleeping quarters, and head. Matthew and the English Captain were seated facing each other across a heavy wooden desk, working on a decanter of claret as they talked.

The English Captain was speaking.

"You have played me the fool, Mister Brock, though I am, as yet, not convinced." Neither was Matthew. "The hypothesis of passage through ages is intriguing. Perhaps some proof is required, or some trial perhaps. Nevertheless, of you, I desire some credentials." He pushed the decanter towards Matthew.

"I believe, sir, that our problem is mutual. I require the same. Until proven otherwise, which is not likely, I remain senior naval officer present." Matthew filled his glass before continuing. "We fly the same ensign, sir. As your frigate is supplicant to a ship of the line, she is also subordinate to *Blackfoot*, dictated by weight, if your will, of armament. I am not convinced that I am the interloper here. Perhaps you are in my century." He took a sip before continuing. He didn't put his glass down. "I will strongly suggest to my captain that we proceed to Halifax. We shall see if it is the fort and harbour of eighteen twelve, or the city and port of nineteen forty-one."

"Damnation, sir! You are most particularly obstinate. It was not I demonstrating uncertainty!" The English Captain stared at Matthew, his face hard. "Exact in time, date and position am I." He sat in silence for a moment. "Agreed, it is to Halifax and her disclosure."

His face softened. "Your behaviour was unacceptable. However, circumstances considered, your behaviour was understandable. Your representation did your commander proud. Of my warrant officers, I'd expect the same."

Tension flowed from Matthew's limbs. He had only done his job to the best of his ability and training. His plea would have been that he was only following orders, and the Old Man would have to support him. But then again, maybe he wouldn't. Maybe he would save his own skin, and sacrifice Matthew in the process. The English Captain surprised Matthew. He considered the man to be an egotistic maniac who would throw away men's lives for the sake of face and honour. Matthew expected he would be forfeit to that pride. Perhaps the Old Man's pride, as well.

"Your patience would be most helpful, sir," continued the English Captain. "Of my duties I have been most neglectful for a boarding party I have sent, under a white flag, to determine the wishes of the *Chesapeake*'s captain. Is he to surrender his vessel or is he to continue our fight. Of what has become of them, I must ascertain, for by this time they should have returned. With your kind permission, sir, this meeting is concluded." He pushed back his chair and stood, took his hat from a peg, and strode out his cabin door, the sentry stamping to attention. Matthew stood, and being careful not to bang his head on the low beams, followed the English Captain to his quarterdeck.

Taking a telescope from near the binnacle, the English Captain studied the *Chesapeake*. He turned and shouted for a Mister Winters.

A lieutenant crossed the quarterdeck from the leeward rail.

"Something is afoot, Mister Winters. Assemble a boarding party ... take the launch. Arm each man with a cutlass and a pistol. Be quick about it!"

"Aye-aye, sir." The lieutenant lifted his hat in salute, turned on his heel and swiftly walked forward, calling out names.

Matthew stared into the gathering gloom at the American frigate. Its sails were furled. Other than that, nothing seemed out of the ordinary. As he watched, the American ensign was lowered and, after a minute, was raised again, only this time with the White Ensign in the superior position. The *Chesapeake*'s captain must have surrendered. The second boarding party was already about a quarter of the distance between the two vessels. He was about to turn away when his eye caught a growing line of white at the bow of the frigate. It looked like a bow wave, but it couldn't be, the vessel's sails were furled. As far as Matthew knew, the vessel certainly didn't have an engine, yet the *Chesapeake* was moving. They must still be in 1941. The English Captain had done a damn good job of pulling the wool over his eyes. He sure had Matthew convinced.

He immediately approached the English Captain, a man who Matthew was starting to admire. He was now having second thoughts.

"This is nineteen forty-one and you know it! This vessel and the one over there have engines. Otherwise, it couldn't move through the water." Matthew was pissed off. "It must have engines. I'll bet this vessel has engines as well."

The English Captain stood with his mouth agape before a visible hue of red began ascending upwards from his neck. It sure didn't signify embarrassment. It signified anger.

"Sir! How dare you? To speak so discourteously to me on my ship is unforgivable! You will not talk to me in such a manner. You speak of this engine. That is not something of which I know."

Matthew directed the English Captain's attention to the American vessel. "The *Chesapeake* is moving without sail, sir. Look!" The bow wave grew as the Chesapeake picked up speed, presenting her starboard quarter gallery. The cutter from the *Shannon* could be seen on a long painter astern of the frigate. It had to have an engine.

Halfway between the two vessels, the lieutenant in command of the boarding party was standing in the stern of *Shannon's* cutter, shaking his sword toward the *Chesapeake*. The oarsmen backed water with their heads turned so they could also see what was happening.

The English Captain was speechless as he stared at the *Chesapeake*. The White Ensign and the American ensign were slowly lowered. Another banner was being raised on the *Chesapeake's* flag halyard. When the flag was broken open, it was barely discernible in the fading light. It was a flag that was foreign to the year 1812. It had a red background upon which was imposed a black cross with white borders. There was a white circle at the junction of the cross and within its circumferance was a feared symbol.

Matthew's hands grew warm, while his body chilled. Again there was a pencil point of fear tracing his spine, not believing nor accepting what his eyes told him. This was one surprise too many. How much more could he take? In his mind he was finally starting to put events together, to link them in a way that made sense, some sense anyway. Well, not really. Now there was a new element, a nasty, dangerous element that blew apart everything he'd constructed in his mind. His whole rationale seemed irrelevant. "SNAFU," a naval saying meaning, "situation normal-all fucked up!" That described him to a tee.

What the flag showed was the feared symbol of the Nazi Party, the Swastika. *Chesapeake* was flying the ensign of the German navy!

CHAPTER 8

▼

"Is it but an illusion? Disbelieve my eyes I must, for what I see is not conceivable." The English Captain sounded quite distressed. He looked at Matthew. "I hope that you are but an apparition, caused perhaps by an unknown blow to my head and recovery is possible."

"It appears," said Matthew, speaking slowly as he considered each word, "That the enemy of my time gives aid to the enemy of your time, that is of course, if we are in your time ... your century. If we are in my time, then it goes without saying that the enemy is ours to share."

"But where is this adversary? Your ship is large. That it is real there is no doubt, although I have not stepped aboard. Perhaps my hand would pass through its side as it would a spectre. The vessel of your enemy is unseen as a phantom is unseen. How do you fight a phantom?"

Gad! If this guy is trying to pull the wool over Matthew's eyes, he is sure playing his part well. Matthew was getting the feeling that *Blackfoot* is the interloper. The more he thought about it, the less doubt he had.

Matthew held out his hand. "Touch me, you will find I am real. My enemy is real, although he is not visible. It is the plague of my time, for the enemy hunts and attacks from below the surface."

The English Captain stared silently at the stern of the *Chesapeake*, apparently for the moment, unable to speak. When he did speak, he spoke slowly, as if fearing the answer.

"Is your enemy ... human?"

Matthew grinned. "Yes, they're human. Although there are many who would say they are not. But that isn't important right now. Would you have any idea as to the destination of the *Chesapeake*?"

"She is out from Boston." The voice of the English Captain betrayed his nervousness.

Seated in the same chair in the English Captain's spacious cabin, another glass of claret sitting on the desk in front of him, Matthew was again in discussion with the English Captain.

"This undersea boat providing impetus to the *Chesapeake*, is this of same design as that patented by Robert Fulton of the United States?"

"Yes, captain … only improved by a hundred and some odd years of development. They must have surveyed the situation and then surfaced near the *Chesapeake* on the side hidden from us. We wouldn't have picked her up on ASDIC, which is one of our defensive systems, since it was probably running at periscope depth. They must have overpowered the Americans and I fear for them. Nazis can be fanatics."

"Nazis?" The English Captain looked puzzled. "Of that country I am not familiar!"

"Nazis are the political masters of Germany. They took power in the early nineteen thirties under a tyrant named Adolf Hitler. It's all very complicated. I just wish our leaders had taken action to stop him at that time."

"Well, you are here, in eighteen twelve. Maybe—"

"What can I do? Write a book? History is history and you can't tamper with that. Just *Blackfoot* being here could change the course of history. If, and I repeat, if we are in eighteen twelve, then I'm sure *Blackfoot* will stay in the background."

"The undersea boat, would it not change history? If it is my year, my future is your history. Both are at great peril as I foresee. If these Nazis side with the Americans in my war, much devastation will befall Canada and Britain."

Matthew took a sip of claret. "You are right! However, my captain will not accept responsibility for the U-boat being here, but I'm sure he will accept the responsibility of hunting it down and destroying it. If it is found to be eighteen twelve, we'll still consider ourselves at war with Germany." He paused a moment. "I guess if it is eighteen twelve, then technically we are at war with the United States!" Holy shit! He couldn't believe he said what he just said. He took a swallow of claret.

"This undersea boat, if a match race was held, at the finish which would be the victor, your vessel or it?"

The English Captain must be thinking of something. Maybe he had an idea. Matthew certainly hadn't thought of one.

"It can do about seventeen knots on the surface, *Blackfoot* can do thirty. They can only do about half their surface speed while submerged."

"You say seventeen knots. Indeed, that is rapid, your vessel even more so." The English Captain drummed his desk with his fingers. "Employing the marked difference, with your kind permission, I entreaty our pursuit. *Shannon* must surpass the *Chesapeake*. We need to employ your vessel in like manner."

"I don't know. It would be my captain's decision of course." Matthew stroked his beard. "All I can do is ask. In the meantime, I would suggest you rig the *Shannon* for towing."

Two hours later, Matthew had his answer. "Halifax can wait, sir. It is to Boston we go, be it the enemy town of eighteen twelve or the friendly city of nineteen forty-one." Matthew paused. "If it is your time, my captain will defer to your authority. I will stay with your vessel. My captain will send over some men to help with our endeavours."

It was dark by the time the other members of *Blackfoot's* company transferred to *Shannon*. Their gear and Matthew's signal gear that included semaphore flags, two Aldis lamps, and a complete flag locker, was hoisted on deck. The crew were made up of Ordinary Seamen Bell and Booth from X-mount, Ordinary Seaman Cripps from A-mount, and Ordinary Seaman Parsons from the port Oerlikon. They were there to handle the tow that *Blackfoot* was passing to the *Shannon*, plus give whatever help required by the English Captain. They reported directly to Matthew who was responsible for communication with *Blackfoot*.

The *Shannon* did not have a bullring so a special rig had to be developed. A ten-inch cable was passed around the circumference of *Shannon*, nipping it with lesser diameter line to the numerous stag-horns, cleats, kevels and timberheads that were the belaying points on the frigate. A large bite was put into the forward end of the cable and seized. The towline was passed from *Blackfoot* and shackled to the bite. Strain was then slowly put on the cable as *Blackfoot* went ahead. HBMS *Shannon* was moving through the water under a power other than sail.

Blackfoot slowly worked up to fifteen knots, both captains unsure of what hull speed *Shannon* would be able to handle. After dawn, a higher speed would be tried. A riding light was suspended from *Shannon's* bowsprit allowing *Blackfoot's* stern lookout to keep a watchful eye on her. On board the *Shannon*, helm orders were relayed from the head back to the helm.

There were eight men posted as lookouts under the watchful eye of the duty lieutenant. The watch on deck sat around the forecastle quietly talking, some taking a "caulk." The ship was unnaturally quiet. There wasn't the constant creaking and groaning of masts carrying a heavy load on a full suit of sails. There wasn't the occasional call to duty for those on watch—the need to adjust tacks, sheets, and braces, or having to cleat or flake down lines. There would be no boson's mates piping all hands on deck, disturbing those off watch and asleep in the hammocks below

Matthew stood by the forward timberheads. It was peaceful. He looked overboard at the foremast chains, then up the shrouds until they disappeared from sight against the stars. He leaned out, looking forward, where the bow wave spread out in a long fan as it ran astern. Phosphorous sharply outlined the edge of each wave.

He absently gave each cannon a pat on its butt as he walked aft. Each touch felt warm. Each touch left a trail of blue light that rapidly disappeared, unnoticed by Matthew. He was aware of an increased heartbeat but chalked it up to all the excitement.

It would be great to see these guns in action. Books he'd read tried to describe in words what it must be like, but Matthew doubted their descriptions were adequate. The sweating men, bandannas over their ears, working the great guns, reaming out the barrels, ramming powder and shot, the gun leaping back on its tackles when fired. He had dreamt of it as a boy.

The realization suddenly hit him, stopping him in his tracks, his heart pounding. His great great uncle is alive at this very moment! Damn it! When did he die?

For some reason, the answer came quickly, his memory calling forth a textbook. Yes! It was his third grade textbook on Canadian history. In his mind he could see its pages and he quickly flipped through it. There was a picture of his famous great great uncle. He remembered it vividly. His mind scanned the page. The writing was simple, written for the skills of a ten year old. Let's see, it was the battle of Queenston Heights. Now the date today is September the twelfth. Holy shit!

His great great uncle had only about a month to live!

CHAPTER 9

▼

The day dawned with the eastern sky slowly brightening before the sun burst forth in brilliance. On deck, Matthew watched as the sun's rays first caught the tops of the masts, highlighting them in stark reality to the deep blue sky above. The rays broke apart as they passed through the rigging, contrasting detail with shadow in an animated cubist composition. The sun was the painter, and the sky the painter's canvas. The sun's warmth was immediately felt when its light reached the deck. It warmed the back of his neck and between his shoulder blades but it couldn't dispel the sadness he felt.

He could only think of his great great uncle and the fact that in less than a month he'd be dead. His famous uncle was a legend that was passed on by his father who learned it from his father, giving the Brock family a pride that could be explained, but couldn't be shared. It was like having a much-loved relative sitting on death row, counting down the days until the trap is sprung, his body drops, and the pre-stretched rope snaps taut. There was absolutely nothing he could do about it, after all, it's history, and history can't be changed, or can it! Perhaps, just perhaps, history can be changed. Matthew reached out with his heart and embraced that hope. It was all he had.

Three quarters of an hour later, Matthew received a message sent by Aldis lamp that *Blackfoot* was to attempt an increase in speed. Matthew informed the duty lieutenant who informed the helm.

The towline lifted from the water and began to tighten, squeezing water from between its strands. *Shannon's* head fell off in a starboard yaw, the two men at her double wheel fought with her, their muscles straining, their teeth set, until she came back on course. This prompted the duty lieutenant to comment that the vessel had a tendency to be a mite cranky.

Shannon's company were mesmerized. Whooping, grinning tars crowded the timberheads, the railing along the top of the beakhead bulkhead, the head area, and the bowsprit. If a sailor had the unfortunate need to piss, he had to do it in a crowd. All through the forward rigging could be seen grinning faces, some of the men wearing scarlet tunics with white cross belts—Britain's Royal Marines—pointing and gesturing with enthusiasm. The petty officers and boson's mates, unable to enforce discipline, allowed themselves to be caught up in the excitement. They were in a party mood, better than hearing the pipe, "Hands to dance and skylark."

One of *Shannon's* midshipmen decided to cast the log, counting the number of knots in the line as it unravelled off the spool. *Shannon*, fifth rate frigate in the Royal Navy of 1812, was ripping through the water at a speed of twenty-one knots.

Matthew; Bell; Parsons; Cripps, and the other members of *Blackfoot's* crew sat back and enjoyed. Booth was with them but he wasn't enjoying much. After trying to eat the breakfast of oatmeal, stale bread, and rancid butter, he'd thrown up through a gun port. The British tars seemed to gulp it down with relish, drinking cups of coffee that had never seen a coffee bean.

"I wonder what they would act like if we got her up to thirty knots," mused Parsons. "I'd give my next piece of tail to see that."

"Your next piece of tail will be your first piece of tail," muttered Booth.

The next day found the *Shannon* under full sail, cruising off the approaches to Boston Harbour. It was the Boston of 1812, not the Boston of 1941, a fact realized by Matthew when they were still over the horizon at dusk. The lights of the modern city would have been reflected by the overcast, since Boston wasn't subject to wartime blackout. *Blackfoot* remained just over the horizon. Matthew was called to the English Captain's cabin. This was just as well, for Matthew had information for the English Captain, information that perhaps the English Captain would not like.

The English Captain looked up from a chart on his desk and signalled Matthew to approach.

"Relax, Mr. Brock." He smiled at Matthew, bent over the chart, and stabbed a spot with his finger.

"The *Chesapeake* and the undersea boat weigh heavily upon me, their disposition I don't know, but must know. You, with one confederate, will put ashore at this spot. You will embark at two bells of the evening watch. Its espionage, if you will, spying, that I require of you, for I am in search of knowledge as to the disposition of the *Chesapeake* and the undersea boat. You are to be clandestine, inquisitive, and analytic. Obtain slops from the purser ... an appropriate disguise, I would think. As to your accent and syntax ... this is why I thought you best for this enterprise. Although it may cause curiosity, English it is not. I have decided upon this evolution myself. Your captain, of course, will be informed. Your return will be no later than midnight tomorrow. I expect your report the following morning. Do you have any questions?"

"No questions, sir, but I do have some information concerning my personal responibilies in this affair. Because the *Chesapeake* is from your time, it goes without saying that she is your responsibility. The undersea boat, however, is from my time and therefore is the responsibility of my captain." He handed a folded paper across the desk. The English Captain stared at the paper, then at Matthew, his eyes showing hostility. Matthew placed the paper on the desk and continued. "These are orders for me from my captain. First, I am to act as liason between yourself and my captain. Of course, while I'm aboard your ship, I will follow your orders."

The English Captain cleared his throat. "That certainly goes without saying." His eyes seemed to bore right through Matthew. He was beginning to look downright hostile.

Matthew swallowed. He was beginning to sweat. "Second, it is my captain's intention to stay out of sight, if that is at all possible. He has charged me with the responsibility of containing the undersea boat to one area where it can be captured or destroyed. That area may be Boston's harbour. If that is not possible, then I am ordered to capture it or destroy it along with her crew. There will be no action taken against the undersea boat without my approval." Matthew pointed to his orders. "All that I just said is written in these orders. Now sir, as to my being a spy, I know nothing about espionage. Hell, I've never even read a mystery novel. However, I also wish to know the disposition of the undersea boat. I will have Ordinary Seaman Bell accompany me, sir.

The English Captain looked at Matthew's orders. He put the finger-tips of his left hand onto the paper and pushed it around. He appeared to be deep in thought. He looked at Matthew, his face softened. "Do you know where *Blackfoot* intends to anchor?"

"I haven't been informed. My captain may decide to anchor in a deserted bay, or perhaps he will cruise out of sight offshore, away from shipping lanes."

"Well, let me know when you know, for to communicate with your captain may at some point be my wish. If he is out of sight, then I will have no way to communicate. Signal flags will be nothing more than useless bunting. Your flashing light method would also be useless. That is a problem that must be addressed."

"That has been taken into consideration, sir. We have a method that will solve your problem. Arrangements will be made after I return from my spy mission."

On hearing that, the English Captain actually smiled. "So Bell is your choice? You know this man is charged with insubordination. I don't have to tell you it's a serious offence."

Matthew felt the tension drain out of him. "Aye, sir, but I believe him to be the best man." Matthew was lying through his hat. He wanted to save Bell from being flogged. Bell's problem was the grog that was issued twice daily, one eighth of a pint each time. He was only nineteen and not used to strong drink, especially pusser rum! His first tot caused him to throw up all over a petty officer's shoes.

To port, the soft light of a harvest moon reflected off waves that broke upon Deer Island's shore. Off the starboard bow, the shoreline of Shirley's Point was just becoming visible. Sitting in the stern sheets of *Shannon's* gig, Matthew thought of his last visit to Boston, under completely different circumstances. He was a tourist, not a spy.

Accompanying Matthew in the gig was Bell, who was suffering from a deserved hangover. He will face the English Captain to answer the charges when they return. *Shannon's* crewmen pulled hard on their oars that were muffled to prevent noise, concentrating on each stroke so as not to catch a "crab." Their course took them across a shoal skirting the south end of Governor's Island before cutting across the shipping channel to the north shore of Dorchester Neck. It was shoal water but the tide and shallow draft of the gig allowed them to stay in the shadows of the shoreline.

Boston of 1812 was a peaceful town in a peaceful setting, situated on a peninsula that is connected to the State of Massachusetts by a narrow strip of land called Boston Neck. It is famous as a revolutionary town, home of the Boston Massacre, the Boston Tea Party, and the birthplace of Benjamin Franklin. It was in this town where the British army, under the command of General Thomas Gage, tried to choke-off the American Revolution by seizing Boston Neck. A good number of veteran minutemen still lived in the town, men who fought at Concord, Lexington, and defended Bunker Hill.

With their history, a great hatred for anything British would be expected, and it would follow that the town would support the war against Canada and Britain. That wasn't the case. They had developed a good relationship with Canadians and a number of Bostonian merchants were lining their pockets with Canadian trade.

It was a pretty town. Its landmarks were the church steeples that served as range markers, guiding storm ravaged ships into her safe harbour. On the opposite bank of the Charles River was the picturesque village of Charlestown.

Boston's harbour was on the east side of the peninsula, between the town itself and Dorchester Neck to the south. As they rowed along the north shore of Dorchester Neck, Matthew squinted into the moonlight towards a long wharf that protruded into Boston's harbour. He could see three tall masts. Hopefully they belong to the *Chesapeake*. If she is there, the U-boat can't be far away. It may be hidden in the shadows at the end of the dock. As they cut around the northwest point of Dorchester Neck, Matthew had the crew rest on their oars for it had been a long pull. Ahead, blocking their path was a low bridge that crossed from Boston to Dorchester Neck. The crew rested and stared toward the town, silent, and listening.

Matthew's focus turned to the town for he needed to find a landing place. There were no lights to be seen. The town seemed to be shut up tight and was eerily quiet.

Perhaps the Nazis had taken over the town!

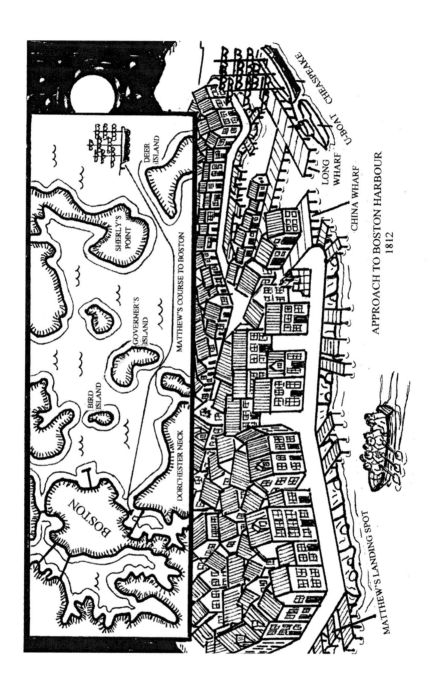

APPROACH TO BOSTON HARBOUR
1812

CHEASPEAKE

U-BOAT

LONG WHARF

CHINA WHARF

DEER ISLAND

SHERLY'S POINT

GOVERNER'S ISLAND

BIRD ISLAND

MATTHEW'S COURSE TO BOSTON

DORCHESTER NECK

BOSTON

MATTHEW'S LANDING SPOT

CHAPTER 10

▼

The full moon had passed its zenith by the time Matthew and Bell reached a small dock on the shore of Boston, across the channel from the tip of Dorchester Neck. They disembarked and walked up the dock to the street. Matthew chose this location because the dock was empty of boats and there was nobody around. There was an empty feeling in the pit of his stomach when he watched the gig pull away. He would see them again at the same place and the same time the next night, if they are there, if he and Bell are still alive.

"Come on, Bell, we'd better get going. This street should take us along the waterfront." He tried to ease the tension. "If I remember correctly, the large dock we could see from the water is called Long Wharf. It's hard to believe, but it still exists in our time." Bell remained silent. Matthew saw him look over his shoulder to where they landed.

The atmosphere of the town was spooky. The moonlight cast ominous shadows across the street. The simple outline of a building took on portentous proportions, sharp roof peaks and multiple chimneys assumed ghostly characteristics. Cast iron roosters and bulls of weather vanes seemed to be twenty times their actual size. All houses were shuttered tight.

"Hold it, Bell!"

Three buildings ahead, two skinny dogs entered into the street, growling and nipping at each other before breaking into a run. They resumed their measured steps, halting when they came to the end of the street. To his right, Matthew saw the large dock that they had rowed silently past to get to their point of embarkation. It was crowded with various styles and types of vessels. To his left was a street that followed the waterfront. "This street follows the shoreline. By following it, we should come to Long Wharf." He began walking. Bell fell in step behind him as if to use Matthew's bulk for protection.

The moon was now well past its zenith. To his left, a door opened slightly, emitting a sliver of light. Someone was watching them, someone who was perhaps very frightened. Matthew didn't know about Bell, but he was scared shitless.

He figured they had to be in a business area of town. The majority of the buildings were constructed of brick, some them two, some of them three stories high. Each building had a wooden sign protruding over the street above the doorway. Each sign had an elegant shape that was embellished with elaborately carved decorations. They passed under the sign for Henderson Finch—Importer of General Goods, and the sign for the Anchor and Crown Tavern which had a detailed carving of a jewelled crown over a carved ship's anchor, boxed on the left by a unicorn and on the right by a lion. There was no boisterous laughter or loud conversation to be heard eminating from the tavern.

Their shadows kept pace as they walked. Matthew kept his eyes peeled for any sign of movement, a mustard seed of fear taking root in his stomach. Everything was quiet. Unnaturally quiet.

They continued north along the dark waterfront, passing many docks of many different widths and lengths. Soon, the moonlight revealed that an old battery, that looked as if it had been undergoing some renovation, blocked their way. There were no guards posted as far as Matthew could determine, just a lot of large stone and stonemason tools scattered about. The street curved to the northwest where only a hundred feet from the battery, another street opened to Matthew's right. The street lead to a wharf that hosted a number of large warehouses, a sign on the first warehouse at the wharf's entrance gave the name "China Wharf."

"Come on Bell, let's go have a look-see." Matthew headed toward the wharf and the waterfront. He found the wharf to be quite wide and it followed the shoreline in a northwest direction. He looked across the harbour. There was the U-boat, moored in front of the *Chesapeake*. It was where they were going and they were almost there. He led Bell quickly along the wharf; his curiosity peaked, for there were no vessels of any kind moored alongside. He found that the wharf didn't connect to what he believed was Long Wharf. They made their way back to the street. It was only a block until they came to the street that led to Long Wharf. At the corner of a brick building with a storefront and sign stating it was a ship's chandler, Matthew halted, indicating with a finger to his mouth, that Bell must remain silent. Tentatively, he approached the corner and looked along the wharf.

It was deserted except for one man who was standing outside a brick building near the shore end of the wharf. He wore civilian cloths and he was holding a musket in a relaxed manner. He was obviously not a German sailor.

Matthew positioned himself where he could watch the man without being seen. He believed the man to be a guard. The guard occasionally lifted his musket and walked to each end of the building to peer down the alleys. What, or who he was guarding, Matthew was determined to find out.

Needing time to think, he motioned for Bell to sit and relax. He must figure out a way to get past the guard and along the wharf. Buildings occupied the north side of the wharf to half its length. There were numerous coils of large diameter line, and stacks of wooden casks. Carts lined the wharf. Some appeared to be empty, while some were full of goods. He crouched, watching the movements of the guard. A short gust of wind lifted leaves and blew them along the wharf, making a light swishing sound. Behind him Bell was asleep, snoring softly, bundled to keep out the autumn chill.

Matthew must have drifted off for he was suddenly conscious that it was daylight. He'd been awakened by the clatter of rushing feet, loud talk, and laughter. Matthew shook Bell awake and hurriedly got to his feet.

"Come on!" yelled a man, motioning for Matthew and Bell to follow.

"What's happening?"

"Our *Chesapeake* has captured that strange boat." The man made a wild gesture toward where the sentry stood. "The crew's locked away in that store room over there. They're to be strung up as the pirates they are and deserve."

"Come on, Bell! Let's follow the crowd." Things couldn't have worked out better.

As they neared the end of the wharf, Matthew noticed that a man in a captain's uniform was mounting the frigate's main shrouds, while holding a speaking trumpet. He was probably the *Chesapeake's* captain. The excited crowd pressed them closer to the frigate. The U-boat was at the end of the wharf, its stern overhung by the *Chesapeake's* bowsprit. There were guards posted along its deck, each packing a musket, each armed with a cutlasses. Matthew could see that they were American sailors. He stared at the U-boat, feeling chilled. So that's the enemy!

A loud explosion startled him, causing him to look toward the *Chesapeake*. A puff of white smoke rose from its seaward side. The Americans must have fired a cannon. The crowd grew silent. The captain raised his speaking trumpet.

"Good citizens of Boston. Return to your homes … I beseech you. It is our misfortune that, for the near future, the undersea boat will remain where it is."

The crowd became more fervent, some questioning what the captain just said about an undersea boat. The captain continued, but with an added threat.

"I say once more … to your homes return, and do so immediately, or order will be enforced!"

With much grumbling the crowd started to disperse, filing in a long line back along the wharf. Matthew tried to hang back by resisting the push of the crowd. He grabbed Bell to keep him near. He'd noticed another man who was trying to attract the attention of the *Chesapeake's* captain. The man had a pale complexion and was quite slim. He was dressed in a handsome top hat with a long cloak draped over his shoulder. He was holding a handkerchief to his mouth.

"You, sir!" yelled the captain who was still on the main shrouds. "To your home or face arrest!"

A man of considerable strength grabbed Matthew's arm. "You heard Captain Lawrence. You want to be arrested?" With Bell at his heels, Matthew followed the man. Before he was out of earshot, Matthew heard the man in the top hat say, "Such talk in a free country."

The moose steak was accompanied by a large boiled potato, along with mounds of carrots and peas that tasted like they were freshly picked from a garden. Everything was covered by rich, thick moose gravy. Matthew found the steak delicious and wolfed it down, helped along by a tankard of rum mixed with water. He was beginning to feel better, his stomach full, his nerves more relaxed. It was his best meal in days—perhaps months.

Matthew pushed his plate away after wiping up the gravy with a hunk of thick bread. He swallowed his last bit of rum and put down the tankard. He patted his extended stomach and burped. With his fingernail, he plucked a string of meat from between two incisors. He signalled to the proprietor of the Sign of the Lamb tavern, who waddled over, his heavy girth causing him to breathe hard.

"Will you accept English money?" The proprietor stared at him, eyes wide. "We jumped from a British ship, you see. Me and me mate here were pressed from a schooner off the coast of Maine. They said we were British citizens." He gave Bell a friendly slap on the shoulder, surprising Bell. "My friend here, Mister Bell, was goin' ta be flogged. We wouldn't have any of that, us being free spirited patriots from a free country, so we stole a gig and jumped ship. We were off Long Island at the time."

The proprietor's eyes brightened, his protruding lips extending into a smile. In fact, he was bloody well beaming! He bent close to Matthew and spoke in a whisper. "Say no more. I'll take English money."

Without warning, the proprietor put his hand on Matthew's shoulder and gave himself a shove up. He stood on the bench, which Matthew could feel was unstable.

"Free Americans!" The crowd in the tavern slowly quieted, their faces turned to stare at the proprietor. "These two men,"—he indicated Matthew and Bell— "These two men ... wrongly pressed off their American vessel by the oppressive arm of John Bull ... are examples of why we're fightin' Madison's war. I know some of you don't agree with it ... but I say our sailors have got to be free from British tyranny. Let's welcome these two heroes!"

The patrons broke into cheers and applause. Matthew stood and bowed in mock appreciation. They'd swallowed his story. He turned to Bell. "Come on! We'd better be on our way."

"Oh ... you're not leavin' yet!" The proprietor signalled to a woman who Matthew figured was the proprietor's wife. She was also quite large. "Martha ... please bring two more tankards for these heroes." He turned to Bell. "These are with my compliments ... and I'll bet there are many others who want to buy you a tankard."

"But ... Dave and I have to leave! We're to rejoin our schooner—"

"You can't be in a rush. Come on ... celebrate your freedom!" The proprietor clasped his hands in front of his apron and smiled happily. "It ain't often I get two genuine American heroes in here." He turned away to serve other patrons.

Bell looked at Matthew and shrugged, picked up his tankard and took a long swig, then wiped his mouth on his sleeve.

"You better be careful with that stuff, Bell. It gets you into trouble."

"I should be able to take it ... ah ... Matthew." Bell smiled. "I've got a full stomach."

One tankard was followed with another; the patrons not letting them leave. Bell was getting happier and happier, louder and louder. Matthew kept interrupting Bell, afraid he might give their charade away. It caused a few curious looks from other patrons.

Oh God! He's going to start singing. Matthew had to take control. Standing, he grabbed Bell by the shirt. "Come on, Bell! We'd better leave."

"Okay, Yeo." Bell struggled to his feet but was quickly shoved back by Matthew when a loud bang was heard. The sound appeared to come from just outside the tavern's door.

Bell sat heavily on the bench, his head lolled forward to hit the table with a thump, just catching the edge of his plate, causing it to wobble. Bell had passed out.

The door of the tavern flew open, and ducking through it, seemingly in a state of panic, came a German naval officer.

CHAPTER 11

▼

Patrons of the Sign of the Lamb tavern stopped talking, stopped drinking, and stopped moving. The German officer, who Matthew could see was a lieutenant, looked frantic, as if not knowing where to go or what to do. His eyes darted here and there, then settled on a number of muskets that the patrons had left leaning against the wall, just inside the door. He grabbed one, cocked it, and ran to the bar. He climbed over it and pressed the muzzle of the musket into the fat stomach of the proprietor, who squealed with fear, and spread his arms in a gesture of surrender.

The German lieutenant looked at the patrons and said something in German, and from his tone of voice, Matthew gathered that he was near panic. A short, stocky man, with a stiff handlebar moustache, stood up, and answered. He spoke in German.

The German lieutenant answered, saying something that must have motivated the man for he slammed his tankard on the table. He quickly moved to grab the remaining muskets just as some American sailors kicked open the door.

The German lieutenant yelled at the man, gesturing wildly with his free hand. The man spoke to the American sailors, this time in English, although with a strong German accent.

"I have to do this! He has George and threatens to kill him, and you all know George is my friend. Don't move, for he is a mean bugger!"

The man, with his arms full of muskets, indicated the entrance to the kitchen and led the German lieutenant, with his hostage, through it.

"Come on," yelled a sailor. "Find some muskets an' let's get after the bastard!"
The tavern quickly emptied of patrons. Outside, from what Matthew could hear,

they were organized into groups. There were a few shouted orders, then the sound of running feet.

Matthew sat where he was, feeling chilled, shocked by what he saw. His alcohol-infected brain was not functioning at full capacity.

He stood and looked at Bell, trying to decide what to do with him. Grabbing him, he laid him on the bench. He felt sorry for the youngster and blamed himself for what happened. He should have pleaded abstinence but instead, allowed the other patrons to feed his ego. He wasn't capable of being a spy. He had been careless, placing himself and Bell in a precarious position. Shit, without help, he wouldn't be able to carry Bell to the rendezvous!

He sat on the opposite bench, elbows on the table, chin resting on his fists. Nothing to do except let Bell sleep it off. He would have to find some other way to get himself and Bell back to the *Shannon*. He looked up; the door to the tavern remained open. Perhaps fresh air would help.

He stood, walked around the table, grabbed Bell by the armpits and lifted the upper part of his body. The bench tipped with a crash when he dragged Bell off it. Matthew dragged him out the door. He sat him on the ground and propped his back against the tavern wall in the warm sunlight. What Bell needed was a mug of kye. Well … perhaps just coffee.

Matthew left Bell and walked through the tavern to its kitchen where a group of women were comforting the proprietor's wife. At his query regarding coffee, one of the women pointed to the large wood-burning stove where a pot of coffee was steaming. The room was uncomfortably hot.

When he returned with a mug of coffee, he found that Bell had thrown up all over the front of his shirt. Shit! How was he going to get the coffee down him? What Bell needed was a cold shower. Hey! That may be just the thing!

Setting the mug down, he began to drag Bell towards a watering trough that was under a hitching rail. It was surrounded by large piles of horse manure. He stopped. There was activity at the warehouse where the Germans were locked up.

Six American sailors came to a halt in front of the sentry. They were accompanied by the pale-faced man with the tall hat and long black cloak who Matthew had seen at the end of the wharf. As Matthew watched, the man handed the sentry a piece of paper. He looked at Matthew and Bell, and then gave Matthew a brief nod and a smile. Perhaps he was showing sympathy for Matthew's situation with Bell. The sentry unlocked the door, stepped aside, and allowed the man to enter.

Matthew continued dragging Bell while keeping one eye on the warehouse. The man left the lock-up accompanied by a German sub-lieutenant; both were engaged in what seemed like animated conversation. The six American sailors did a right turn and marched off, followed by the man in the tall hat and the German officer. Matthew, still hanging onto Bell, watched them go. They were heading along the wharf towards the *Chesapeake* and the U-boat.

"Maybe our job isn't finished, Bell!"

He felt the back of his legs come in contact with the watering trough. He sat Bell down with his legs in a pile of manure. Turning Bell over, he hung him face down over the filthy water. He grabbed Bell's hair.

"This is going to hurt me more than it's going to hurt you." That's what his mother used to say as she was about to apply a stick of kindling to his posterior. He hurt a lot. For some reason, his mother didn't seem to feel a thing. He pushed Bell's head under water, held it there for a few seconds, and then pulled it up. Nothing!

Again he immersed Bell's head. This time, when Bell's head emerged, he was coughing and sputtering, spitting the dirty water out of his mouth and nostrils. Matthew slapped him on both sides of the face. A chief petty officer shouldn't slap an ordinary seaman but these were extraordinary circumstances. Bell struggled to a sitting position before falling over sideways to empty the contents of his stomach.

"Gad, you must've been a difficult child." He grabbed Bell under the arms. "Here ... stand up and lean on me. Let's get some coffee into you!"

While feeding Bell the coffee, Matthew watched as the man and the German sub-lieutenant stood on the wharf in front of the U-boat and talked. The German gestured with his arms and occasionally pointed at something on the vessel. Then, after climbing the conning tower to the U-boat's bridge, they disappeared from sight. Were the Americans only curious, or were they up to something? Matthew was unsure of what was required of him. He could just shrug, get Bell on his feet and able to walk, and then head back to the rendezvous with the *Shannon's* gig. Nobody would be any the wiser. He was of two minds. Years of naval discipline had given him a strong sense of duty, which pulled him in the direction of staying. He decided to leave—no—fug it! The U-boat was his responsibility so he'd better check it out.

"Stay put, Bell." Matthew entered the empty tavern and took a half-full bottle of rum—at least it had better be rum! He pulled the cork and sniffed it. It was rum all right. He dropped the cork to the floor. He had to act the part of a drunk, think the way a drunk would think. He gripped the bottle. The bottle is your best friend, and you can't let go of your best friend. He left the tavern, noted that Bell was asleep, then Bell was forgotten, he had to play the role. He made his way along the wharf, grabbing onto barrels and coils of line to steady his walk. He wondered if he should start singing, but decided against it.

He staggered and fell hard against a large coil of line, making sure as a drunk would, that he didn't spill any rum. He tipped the bottle to his mouth but didn't swallow a drop. At the same time, he allowed himself to slide to a seated position. He let some rum dribble down the front of his shirt. Using his free hand he pulled himself to a standing position and continued to stagger along the wharf. He could see that the American sentries were eyeing him with curiosity and humour. He held the bottle towards them. Like any good drunk, he was willing to share.

One of the Americans came to where Matthew stood and grabbed hold of the bottle. He tried to snatch it away but Matthew held on and a tug-of-war ensued. He pretended to lose his grip as he staggered and sank to one knee, holding both hands toward the bottle, his face expressing concern. The American laughed. He dropped his arms and took on a sad look as if realizing he'd lost the bottle for good.

"Get lost ol' man. You don't need any more."

"But ... I come tuh see yuh. Yer mah friend. Yer all mah friends ... aren't you? An' friends share ... don't they?"

"Aye, friends share. Then you won't mind sharin' with me other friends, will you."

Matthew stood and slapped the man on the shoulder, leaned on him for support, with what he hoped was a silly grin on his face. Then he stood stalk still, his mouth and eyes wide open, acting as if he'd suddenly discovered the U-boat.

"Hey! What sort'a boat is this?" He left the American and walked toward the U-boat on unsteady legs. Behind him, the Americans were sharing the bottle. Now, he just had to get aboard—but he was too late.

The head and shoulders of the man with the tall hat appeared above the bridge screen. At first he didn't see Matthew. He was looking down, perhaps paying attention to his footing. He stood upright with his back to Matthew and yelled something, in German, directed at the hatch. The head and shoulders of the German sub-lieutenant appeared.

Matthew turned and began to walk quickly back along the wharf.

"Hey! You there! Stop where you are!"

Matthew quickened his pace.

CHAPTER 12

▼

Shit! That was a stupid mistake!

"Come on, Bell! Let's get the hell out of here!" Matthew grabbed Bell by the arm and hauled him to his feet. Bell stood blinking at him. He dragged him by the arm. "That man is coming after us!" Bell fell to his knees.

"Shit!"

The man was almost up to them. Matthew clenched his fists. He hadn't been in a fist fight since basic training, but it looked like he may have to use his fists now. The man noticed the clenched fists and stopped ten feet away, holding both hands in front of him in a gesture of apparent good will.

"I mean you no harm," said the man, "For a gentleman I am ... although the curiosity I find in myself may diminish said claim." He looked at Bell who was struggling to his feet, then back at Matthew. "It is your regard for my business that is the source of my curiosity, for greatly is spying frowned upon. If I may be so bold as to inquire, sirs, as to your names, and more importantly, your nationality?"

"Dave and I are mates and patriotic Americans, as if it were any of your business," said Matthew, not taking his eyes off the man. "We jumped from a British frigate after being wrongly pressed."

"Sir! Your intelligence I respect until shown otherwise, so I request return in kind." The man looked him up and down. "As sailors you are clothed but sailors you are not."

"Yes we are—"

"And Hell is but a pleasant abode where argument will lead us … so … direct we must be. Sailors you are, allow that benefit I will, but to a sailing vessel you are strangers for your hands speak in volumes."

Matthew looked at his hands. What the hell was this guy on about? Bell must be coming around for he was looking at his hands as well.

"A sailor is exposed by the black of his hands, for no matter the stiffness of brush or how vigorous the scrub, the tar will not wash off." The man smiled. He had them dead to rights and Matthew knew it.

"It is my experience,"—the man indicated, with his hand, the Sign of the Lamb tavern—"that the best conversations are held in comfort and since that is my hope, refreshment I will gladly provide."

Matthew thought quickly but he also thought differently. Perhaps an opportunity had presented itself. He may be able to get more information from this man, whoever he is, information that may be valuable to him and his responsibility for the U-boat.

"Ahh … thanks … we'd be honoured … but we'd both prefer coffee. I think my mate here will agree to that."

"Coffee may be had there." The man turned to lead the way, not looking back to see if Matthew and Bell were following.

The bastard's pretty cock-sure of himself.

The tavern was still empty of patrons. The man chose a table in a corner farthest from the door and sat down, not saying anything, only coughing occasionally into a handkerchief. The man didn't look well. Matthew helped Bell to the bench across from the man and sat down.

"Two coffees and ale for me," said the man to the proprietor's wife who came from the kitchen, wiping her face on a large towel. The man didn't speak until after the order was brought. He swallowed a mouth full of ale, placed the tankard on the table, and then stared directly into Matthew's eyes.

"If I am wrong, you may call me an ass, but Canadians you are, and if I may be so bold, not of this century. It is the iron-sided steam-powered naval vessel from which you come, for just over the horizon she sails."

Matthew sputtered, spitting coffee onto the rough boards of the table. This man had him dead to rights.

"Listen … I have been impolite in not introducing myself, nor have I allowed the opportunity for you to do likewise. I have a professional interest into the power of steam. You have heard of me perhaps? My name is Fulton. Robert Fulton."

"Well I'll be damned," said Matthew. He was getting excited. "You built the first steam vessel."

"Your servant, sir." Fulton gave Matthew a nod. "For the first diving vessel I also claim credit. My interest in the diving vessel under the fortunate command of Captain Lawrence of the *Chesapeake* goes without saying." He took another swig of ale, wiping his mouth on his sleeve. "As to your spying on me, I can understand, for the German is your enemy ... as technically you are mine ... a matter which I intend to overlook ... for now."

That's it! Fulton must have got all his information about *Blackfoot*, and the fact that they were Canadian, from the German sub-lieutenant—or perhaps the American Captain who had seen *Blackfoot* first hand. It was doubtful that the American Captain would know they were Canadian. Matthew looked at Fulton over the rim of his coffee mug. The man must be sick for his face is quite pale, and he's also dabbing his mouth continually with a handkerchief.

Fulton leaned back and placed his hands flat on the rough boards of the table. "For a proposal I wish to make of which your consideration will be appreciated."

Matthew waited.

"My interrogator or agent you must be, for to communicate with your captain is my ambition. A question I have which you will ask for me. As you say, my name is credited with the invention of steam power ... to reduce in respect Mister James Watt is not my intention ... however, I applied its use to maritime vessels and yours, sir, is the epitome of my endeavours. It would give me great prof ... ah ... satisfaction to see what fruit the seed I have planted bears in the future."

Fulton looked seriously at Matthew.

"It is your decision, but I'd be most thankful for your efforts on my behalf, in requesting of your captain his hospitality, for I must see your ship!"

Matthew nodded. God! If he could only think straight! "I can only ask."

"Good. Say tomorrow ... or the day after? A prompt answer would be appreciated." He patted the table. "Here is where I will await your captain's reply. It will be a positive one, I'm sure."

Fulton swallowed the last of his ale. "Listen, it is to your ship you are now returning. Is there any assistance that you require? Tell me, where is your boat so that I can direct you to it?"

Matthew hesitated. "I'm afraid I can't tell you that, sir!"

"It's as I should have expected. Very well, I shall say my good-byes." Fulton stood up.

Matthew had a sudden thought, a thought so far out in left field that it surprised him. It must have dwelt in the back of his mind for it burst forth in all its clarity. He put up his hand to stop Fulton.

"I have a request of you, sir. Perhaps you can be my agent for I have a message to send, but have no means to send it."

"If help I can give you, I'd be most happy to assist."

"Thank you. Would you happen to know of anyone who is leaving for the Niagara? Perhaps that someone could carry a message for me? It is a message to a relative ... who I am greatly concerned about!"

"Why yes, a man I know leaves in two days. A favour is owed me by this man so I most certainly can help."

"Good. I need a pen and some paper."

"Of course. A pen and some paper I will fetch from the proprietor."

Matthew was handed a course paper, a bottle of smelly ink, and a pen carved from a large white feather. Holding his tongue between his teeth he laboriously wrote his note. He only blotted it a couple of times. He folded it and sealed it with a drop of hot wax from a stick of wax that Fulton had pulled from his pocket and melted over a candle. He addressed the note and handed it to Fulton, who immediately read the address. It was addressed to Major General Isaac Brock, Fort George, Niagara.

Fulton looked at Matthew, eyes wide.

"A relative you said? What, pray, is your name?"

"My name is Matthew Brock! Matthew Isaac Brock!"

CHAPTER 13

▼

It looked to Matthew that Ordinary Seaman Bell was one happy sailor. His punishment for insubordination was stoppage of grog for one week. There would be no "cat-of-nine-tails" at the grating. Matthew was also greatly relieved. He had seen it before. Old salts considered it a hard punishment. Grog was part of a sailor's routine and a valued tradition. It bonded men with their mates and helped to forge a ship's company. The navy would fall apart without it. It was a form of currency on the lower deck, so and so owed another mess member "sippers" in payment for a favour. Although illegal to do so, grog was hoarded. Clandestine parties, that usually involved gambling, could be found in some hidden corner on a Saturday evening at sea.

Matthew explained to the English Captain, Bell's complete innocence with alcohol. He pointed out that Bell was under twenty-one years of age and in his navy, grog was withheld until a seaman reached that age. In fact most countries by the nineteen forties didn't allow drinking until the age of twenty-one.

The English Captain was astonished. "Very oppressive! The nineteen forties would not be to my liking!" His face expressed sadness, and from what Matthew could see, a sadness that was truly felt. When the English Captain passed the sentence of stoppage of grog, the offended petty officer tightened his lips and nodded his approval.

Earlier, before Bell's hearing, Matthew completed in writing, his report on the mission. He made two copies, one for the English Captain, and the other copy he kept for the Old Man. Later in the day, at two bells of the afternoon watch to be exact, Matthew was summoned to the English Captain's cabin. Across from him, the English Captain was drumming his fingers on his desk, seemingly deep in thought.

"It was a credible case you argued on behalf of Seaman Bell."

"Er ... thankyou, sir."

"The success of your mission, of course, moderated my justice. Now I wish to question you as to your knowledge of Mister Robert Fulton. What is said of him in your century?"

"Only that he was a great inventor, sir. He is credited with building the first steam-powered vessel."

"Well, the man is a mercenary and a rogue. It is to the highest bidder, with no allowance given to nation or cause, that he sells his devilish inventions. Profit is his motive and profit he will gain by way of his tour of the undersea boat. I see no good coming of it!"

"He's asked permission to tour *Blackfoot*, sir."

The English Captain stiffened. "That I know, for it is written in your report."

"I imagine the captain of the *Chesapeake* told him of *Blackfoot*."

"Have nothing to do with him, I beseech you! Your technology, by his hand, would be turned against us. The conquest of Canada by the United States and the subjugation of Europe to the yoke of Napoleon would be the result, for sell it he will to both our adversaries. Over your ship I have no authority, but refuse him your captain must. This I say as senior naval officer present!"

That was an order that Matthew agreed with.

The English Captain's mood suddenly changed, Fulton seemingly forgotten.

"Of the undersea boat I am gravely concerned! For the Americans, the vessel is advantageous. It is a most powerful weapon that it could turn the tide of this war to their favour. They need only fathom its use to make it a threat."

"I doubt if they can, sir. They don't have the knowledge required. The only way I can see ..." Matthew looked at the skylight. How should he phrase it? "They might form an alliance with the Nazis. I can't see it myself. The Nazis can't be popular after having taken a hostage. If you don't mind me saying so, sir, I was quite surprised when I found that the U-boat was in American control. I'd naturally assumed the Nazis had control of the *Chesapeake*."

"The superiority of technology would, I suppose, quite naturally by you be assumed. Guilty I am of equal sin, for in fretting about the undersea boat; I'm failing to consider ingenuity, which can win battles, as Nelson showed over and over again. The Americans are very apt in that regard, as shown in their last war which gained them independence. It is a cause for concern, that I must say."

"I know! They are very creative with their history."

"To what do you refer?"

"Oh … they claim to have won the battle for Bunker Hill." Matthew was originally thinking of the battle of New Orleans, a battle where the Americans claim to have won the War of 1812, a battle that hadn't yet taken place. He had to think of something else in a hurry. "Don't fire until you see the whites of their eyes and all that rot."

"Of the battle for Bunker Hill I am somewhat familiar. As to eyes, and the whiteness thereof, it bears no sense whatever, except perhaps, some general's verbal intercourse that over time has gained significance beyond its worth."

Matthew nodded. *He doesn't know how close to the truth he is.*

The English Captain pushed back his chair, stood, and walked to the stern window to look at the dark form of *Blackfoot*. The Old Man had brought the destroyer closer to shore and was following in the *Shannon's* wake. He wasn't showing any running lights, or light of any kind. He motioned Matthew to join him.

"I am convinced that the *Chesapeake's* captain's intention is to utilize the undersea boat. And Fulton, I believe, will have his hand in it." The English Captain bent to pick a dead leaf from one of the potted plants that lined the window seat. "He needed permission of the *Chesapeake's* captain to tour that vessel." He twirled the leaf between two fingers as he looked at Matthew. "The stage is set. The curtain has risen. It is you and your captain's cue, and at centre stage you both must now stand. The undersea boat must be destroyed."

Matthew followed the English Captain's gaze. *Blackfoot* was a beautiful ship, even at night. She could be seen outlined against the clouds, the bow-wave a white check on a blackboard sea.

"I will see what I can do, sir?"

Three hours later, Matthew was back in the English Captain's cabin.

"Sir, I am not convinced that the Americans could, or would, use the undersea boat. I believe that the American's would not trust the Nazis. However, this is my plan, and since it involves the use of *Blackfoot*, my captain has approved it and will do whatever needs to be done to see it a success. With your permission, sir, *Shannon* will draw out the *Chesapeake* by presenting herself as a tempting target. The *Chesapeake's* captain must see an advantage for him to leave his safe harbour." Matthew paused, expecting a comment from the English Captain.

"Pray continue." The English Captain wasn't showing any emotion.

"*Blackfoot* will remain hidden. No ironclad vessel will appear in American history books. As the *Chesapeake* makes her way out from Boston Harbour, the

Shannon will act as a spotter for *Blackfoot's* shells. The undersea boat will be destroyed." Matthew watched as various expressions played on the English Captain's face. He smiled.

"By God's grace, *Chesapeake* will also be my prize. By what method will we communicate with the hidden *Blackfoot?*"

"As I said before, sir, we have a method that will serve what is required," said Matthew, not taking his eyes off the English Captain's face.

"If that is so, then to use my ship to our advantage will be my quest."

HBMS Shannon greeted the dawn cleared for action. She was tacking up Broad Sound intending to take position just west of Long Island. It was the English Captain's intention to anchor from both the stern, and the bow, in five fathoms, in clay bottom. *HMCS Blackfoot* was already in position just east of Outer Brewster, anchored in seven fathoms.

Shannon was to be in position by 1100 hours, that is, if the breeze held. It was blowing from the northwest, the direction she wanted to go, which necessitated multiple tacks. She was just east of Green Island at sunrise. The sailing master calculated that unless the wind backed to the northeast, it would take nine more tacks.

Blackfoot's diesel cutter was angling to intercept *Shannon.* The spray kicked up by the cutter's bow prevented Matthew from identifying the occupants, but he knew the cargo it carried. It took thirty minutes for the cutter to come alongside *Shannon.* A crate was lifted on deck where Matthew took charge of it. The cutter let go of the main chains and steered for *Blackfoot.*

The boards were hammered off the crate to reveal a portable wireless. It took over two hours to rig the aerial. Insulators were attached to both the main and mizzen mast, the wire aerial was then strung between the two. Matthew made his first trip up the shrouds to supervise Ordinary Seamen Booth, Parsons, and Cripps, who performed the various tasks. Now it was time to test the set. He checked the frequency setting, and then he picked up the hand held microphone.

"*Blackfoot, Blackfoot, Blackfoot* ... this is *Shannon, Shannon, Shannon* ... radio check ... over."

"*Shannon* ... this is *Blackfoot* ... roger ... out."

Radio contact was established. Matthew looked up for the first time since firing up the set. He found himself surrounded by sailors. Some had their mouths open; others had wide, toothless grins. They were all staring at the wireless. One was digging out his ears with his forefingers, seeming in disbelief of what he was hearing.

Matthew couldn't help but smile. These men know nothing about electronics. To them, the wireless would be a magic box.

CHAPTER 14

▼

Above Matthew the sails luffed as *Shannon* began to tack through the wind. All hands were tailing sheets, tacks, and braces. Tacking a square-rigger in light winds was a tricky operation, the officer of the watch had to time his orders perfectly or the frigate would wind up in irons. This would necessitate the tricky process of wearing ship, with no room to manoeuvre. The English Captain was determined that this would be the second last tack, in spite of objections from the master. *Shannon* approached the shoal that ran southeast, starting from the north end of Long Island. *Shannon* had to head north to just west of Deer Island before tacking to bring the wind onto the starboard beam for a clear course to the anchorage.

The yards groaned against their parrels, pulled around by the braces to catch the wind as it swung to the port side. Petty officers, at their stations for tacking, yelled their orders. "Stamp an' go, stamp an' go. Haul weather braces ... check away looward! A tad more on that sheet there! Ease off that tack yah scurvy tits." The deck was in orderly confusion.

Matthew, who was trying to keep out of the way beside the mizzen, was watching the action. The mast shuddered, shifting a good foot aloft, as the leeward shrouds became weather shrouds. He could make out Ordinary Seaman Bell who was sitting on the trustle tree. It was his job to spot the fall of shot from *Blackfoot* and call down corrections. Matthew would relay these corrections to *Blackfoot* on the portable wireless. Bell appeared to be hanging on for dear life. *Shannon* settled onto the port tack and continued on a northerly course for the next fifty-five minutes.

Shannon tacked for the last time, a full hour behind schedule. Forward, the crew at the cathead let the bower anchor hang "a'cock bill," ready to drop on order.

The English Captain was on the quarterdeck to observe the naval ritual of "noon." The officer of the watch checked the chronometer, which was contained in a protective wooden box, and said, "Noon, sir!" The English Captain nodded and said, "Make it so!" The boson's mate rang eight bells. It was now a brand new day on board *HMBS Shannon*. The duty midshipman prepared to cast the log.

"Ahoy on deck! Ahoy on deck!"

Matthew recognized the voice of Bell and looked up. Bell had a speaking trumpet and was making use of it.

"The U-boat's not in position! I say again, the U-boat is not in position! It was there when I last looked but she's not there now!"

The English Captain lifted his hat, wiped his forehead and looked at the sun. He slapped his hat against his leg.

"It is as I feared, though my heart held hope, though false it was, that Fulton would not succeed." He walked to the weather rail. "Damn his eyes!"

Shannon would have been in a good position, anchored fore and aft with a spring rigged between the cables. She would become a floating battery, able to point her guns through ninety degrees by adjusting the fore and aft cables. *Chesapeake* would be restricted in her ability to manoeuvre, boxed in by the Middle Ground, Spectacle Island, and Deer Island. *Shannon* would be able to inflict heavy damage from a full broadside long before the *Chesapeake* could bring her broadside into action.

"Ahoy on deck! U-boat bearing green five oh!"

Matthew pointed in the right direction. The English Captain stood still, the sun highlighting the lighter strands of his red hair. The veins on each side of his neck betrayed his anxiety. There are some things that aren't easily hidden and a wildly beating heart is one of them.

"There is still a chance. I can still use my hidden weapon." He turned to the duty midshipman. "The chart, it is on my desk. Fetch it."

"Aye-aye, sir." The midshipman disappeared below.

"Re-cat the anchor! Stand by to tack! Load with ball and run out the guns!" The *Shannon* had already cleared for action. The midshipman appeared with the chart. The English Captain laid the chart on the deck where he plotted the coordinates of the U-boat. He wrote them on a slate and handed them to Matthew who called *Blackfoot* on the wireless and passed the news of the U-boat, her coordinates, and estimated course and speed.

Shannon's company were manning the tacks, sheets, and braces, standing patiently but nervously, waiting for the shouts and pipes of boson's mates. The sky above them was suddenly ripped apart with a sound like tearing canvas, prompting the master to glance nervously at the sails. Matthew, trying to focus an ancient telescope, watched for the fall of shot. The lens was suddenly filled with large columns of water, obscuring the U-boat. When the water settled, the U-boat was still there only its shape was altering. A large mass of birds rose in a confused cloud from a small island just north of the vessel.

Cripps relayed Bell's new coordinates. "Up twenty five, two degrees starboard!" Matthew passed the information on to *Blackfoot.*

"Helm alee! Check away slowly weather braces an' sheets." *Shannon* was tacking. The sky was again ripped apart. *Shannon's* bow was directly into the wind, pointing at the U-boat. From his spot on the quarterdeck, Matthew was unable to observe the fall of shot.

"*Blackfoot* has the range! Target zigzagging! Port four degrees!" It was only a minute before the third salvo was passing overhead.

"Possible hit! U-boat beam-on! Heading south! Port two degrees!" The fourth salvo passed overhead. It straddled the U-boat. When the water settled, the U-boat was heading back toward Boston's harbour.

"Target retiring!" said Cripps. "And … what's that? Say again?" Cripps was looking up the mast to where Bell had a telescope focused on the U-boat. "There appears to be two men fighting on the conning tower. Range up fifty, two degrees starboard." Again, Matthew forwarded the information to *Blackfoot.*

The English Captain tucked his telescope under his arm and climbed the mizzen weather shrouds to just below the futtocks. He put the telescope to his eye. Above him, *Blackfoot's* fifth salvo made its angry passage. Matthew braced his telescope against the mizzen to steady it. When the columns of water subsided, the U-boat was still on course for Boston's harbour. Only one man remained on the conning tower. In the U-boat's wake was the head and shoulders of a man who was waving frantically at the man in the conning tower. The U-boat proceeded on course. After two minutes, the man gave up and began swimming for the small island with all the birds.

"Heave to! Lower a cutter! Arm detail with musket and cutlass!" The English Captain called out the orders as he descended the shrouds. Matthew radioed *Blackfoot* to cease firing.

It took fifteen minutes to lower the cutter, rig the mast, and man her. Matthew climbed into the cutter as commander of the task. The sail was raised and the cutter tacked toward the island. Being fore and aft rigged, the cutter pointed a lot higher than *Shannon*, and took only one and a half hours to make the island. The man stood on the rocky beach, watching them approach.

As the whaler grounded on the beach, the crew leapt over the gunwales, their pistols held high to keep the priming dry. Matthew walked to the bow and watched the man approach with his hands spread in a gesture of greeting.

"A fine afternoon, is it not, Mister Brock? Meeting you again gives me great pleasure, though your word I expected earlier. Tell me, Mister Brock, your captain's answer. It was positive, I hope?"

CHAPTER 15

▼

"I must say that I'm quite angry with you, Mister Fulton." Matthew kept an eye on a small cutter making its way down channel from Boston Harbour. "It is hard for me not to believe that you commandeered the undersea boat and that you were taking it to sea to destroy the *Shannon.*"

Robert Fulton was engrossed in the activities going on around him. Appearing to be startled by Matthew's comment, his face took on an aggrieved look. "I obtained permission to take said vessel to sea from Captain Lawrence. I wanted to learn more about its method of propulsion and its systems."

"That's what I am afraid of, Mister Fulton. By destroying the *Shannon,* you would learn about the undersea boat's weapon systems. It would make you rich, and also make you a national hero. A man with an inventive mind such as yours would surely profit from the knowledge you would have gained. It would throw a wrench, if you will, into the rhythm of time itself. Nothing should come before its time, Mister Fulton. This is how the world keeps in balance. Too much weight on one side will cause unknown effect on the other. This worries me, Mr. Fulton. In fact, you and your desire to take advantage of my ship and me is a constant worry. I can tell you this, right now! You will not get a tour of my ship. Not if I can help it. You have probably learned too much already with your voyage on the undersea boat."

"Of the undersea boat, I learned nothing. I was being shown the interior of the vessel the day of your spying, but all I saw was levers, guages, and pipes. Of these levers, gauges and pipes, the German officer, Lieutenant Godt, would not inform me. Meeting you quelled my frustration, for opportunity I did see. As to your ship, I will get a tour. On that you can count."

"I believe your frustration will return, Mister Fulton, for you will not get a tour. However, yesterday when you made the voyage on the undersea boat, you must have learned a good number of things." Matthew looked Fulton in the eye. He wanted the truth.

"It was the same Lieutenant Godt. Captain Lawrence released half of the German crew, on promise of their return, with the mission to attack and sink this vessel here—the *Shannon*. I was avid in my plea to be included. I explained to Captain Lawrence, that with the knowledge I would gain, he would soon have a fleet of undersea boats at his command. On exiting the harbour, Godt informed me that he was dropping me off on Bird Island and he was setting his course for Prussia, his commander and the rest of the crew be damned! So determined was he that he swore to endure your shellfire. To fight him was my only recourse. I am talking here with you today because pugilism is beyond my capabilities and health."

He stared at Matthew. "To the question I observe in your mind, the answer is no. I was not allowed below. The knowledge desired by my heart was kept from me."

A weight was lifted off Matthew's shoulders. He believed that Fulton was truthful and the near future is still safe from the scourge of U-boats.

They stood in silence, staring at the scene that passed as *Shannon* picked up speed on a broad reach. In the short period *Shannon* had been blockading the harbour, a number of coastal traders were seen making their way through the islands, taking advantage of high slack, and the start of the ebb tide.

Shannon just completed her inward leg and was wearing to bring the wind to the aft port quarter to run back out to Broad Sound. Every day for almost a week, the *Shannon* came in sight of the people of Boston, sailing in on the flood and out on the ebb, all the while, the *Chesapeake* sat at the end of Long Wharf, seemingly impotent.

Matthew changed the subject. "Where is the *Constitution*?"

Fulton suddenly realized he was being spoken to, although he didn't appear to hear Matthew's question.

"Excuse me, for I was deep within my thoughts and heard naught of what you said, of which, I ask of you to kindly repeat."

"I asked you where the *Constitution* was."

"I assume you mean the frigate. Last of her that I've heard, and I'm not well informed on her movements, is that Philadelphia was her last port of call. Boston welcomed Captain Hull and the *Constitution* and celebration of her victory over the British frigate *Guerriere* resulted in a large gathering. Sadly, I was not in Boston at the time, for eat most heartily with much libation did both sailor and town's folk, to be sure."

"The *Constitution* is quite famous. The American capacity for bull … er … you know, the American … how can I say it,"—Matthew patted a timber head as he collected his thoughts—"Americans have their own version of this war as do Canadians. Americans, you know, have a ravenous capacity for cultivating heroes, many of them from this war. The *Constitution* becomes America's answer to Briton's famous wooden walls. I've seen her! I visited Boston a few years ago … you know … during the nineteen thirties. I was on a courtesy visit with the Royal Canadian Navy."

Fulton raised his eyebrows, an indication of his interest. "I must say that amazed I am that after one hundred years and more, she still floats!"

"Yes, she's preserved as a museum piece at dockside in Boston." Matthew looked toward Boston, the image of the city she became pictured in his mind. He swept his hand indicating the area from Dorchester Neck to Noodles Island. "You know, you wouldn't recognize the place."

Fulton's eyes took on a distant look, perhaps trying to visualize a Boston of the next century. Matthew doubted that he could envision it.

"A vibrant town she must be for she has within her the seed of greatness." Fulton turned away from Matthew, put his hands behind his back, and slowly walked away, seemingly deep in thought.

Matthew's thoughts turned to his great great uncle who, at this moment, was a living, talking, thinking human being. He wasn't sure why he'd written the note. Perhaps it was from a deeply rooted sense of duty, a family loyalty that had existed for generations. His father, his grandfather, and great grandfather, had all travelled to Queenston where the statue of his great great uncle adorned the top of a tall column. Part of the family fortune went into its rebuilding after it was blown up by some idiot activist.

Actually, it was hard for Matthew to put a finger on his feelings about his famous ancestor. In school he talked of him with tremendous pride, calling him a Canadian hero. His father spoke of him as a man who walked his own road, proving that determined action brings profitable results. He said that there are two types of men in the world, those that lead and those that follow, and Uncle Isaac was a leader. His father made the same sacrifice for his country as his great great uncle, that being his life, his future, somewhere on a battlefield in Belgium.

Matthew's thoughts were interrupted by the hale of the masthead lookout. The cutter Matthew had observed earlier had raised a white flag indicating a wish to parley. Appearing on deck, the English Captain studied the cutter though his glass. After conferring with the master, he ordered the *Shannon* to heave to.

Shannon swung through the wind onto the starboard tack before drifting to a stop, her main sails backed against the mast counteracting the draw of the fore and mizzen sails. The cutter dropped its sails and came alongside.

Matthew recognized the man as soon as he stepped through the entry port. He may have been under the influence of alcohol at the time but the episode was fresh in his memory. The short, fat man with the large handlebar moustache approached the English Captain and gave a stiff bow, at the same time, clicking his heels together. Before he could introduce himself, the English Captain strode past him to the entry port where the English lieutenant that was being held aboard *Chesapeake* was making his appearance. The lieutenant lifted his hat and reported himself aboard and fit for duty.

The short, fat civilian seemed a bit nervous, running his hands through his hair and wiping his mouth on his sleeve. He stiffened as the English Captain returned his attention to him.

"Ulrich von Friedeburg at your service, sir, and I humbly bestow kindest regards from Captain Lawrence of the United States Frigate *Chesapeake*. He has entrusted me with important information which he wishes … if you so wish … that you look upon as urgent. Captain Lawrence also makes known what he believes should be the appropriate action with certain requests of you, realizing of course, that he is asking much of your good will. To show his faith, he has released to your service, without parole … your good lieutenant." Von Friedeburg extended his hand.

"You are most welcome, Mister von Friedeburg. I sincerely hope that my hospitality you won't find lacking." The English Captain ignored the proffered hand. "Express, if you will, on my behalf, my gratitude to Captain Lawrence for his release of my lieutenant." He indicated the companionway. "Pray come this way, for you look in need of refreshment. You are most frightfully bruised! The sad result of an unfortunate accident, to be sure. Please indulge me, sir, for I'm most curious."

Matthew was surprised and excited when informed by a midshipman that he was wanted in the English Captain's cabin. It had to be news of the escaped Nazi officer.

"Ahh, Mister Brock, come in, be seated." The English Captain indicated a chair. "Let me present Mister von Friedeburg of the town of Boston."

"I visited your town just the other day. Is this an official visit, Mister Friedeburg?" Matthew shook the friendly hand that was offered.

"Yes, I recognize you! An American hero, you were … although counterfeit to be sure … and a good task of it you made. As to this visit—"

The English Captain signalled his servant. "Have some refreshment Mister Brock, for the duration of this meeting, I fear, will try us all."

Matthew accepted the offering. It was claret. He settled back in his chair, the pleasantries over with. The English Captain nodded to the German.

Von Friedeburg began to tell his story.

"He is an evil man!"

"You mean the German officer?" said the English Captain.

"Yes, sir. He is a dangerous lunatic! His intelligence is beyond question and that's what makes him a danger. He is a man with persuasive influence, a man focused on a singular ambition. He has declared himself Fuehrer, and he wishes to subjugate this nation."

"What is this man's name?"

"His name is Klaus Hartenstein."

"Please proceed, Mister von Friedeburg."

"Destiny's plan, according to him, placed him in the perfect country … the United States. The drowning death of his commanding officer … unable to come to his aid, he said … also helped."

Of course! The commanding officer was the wounded man who drowned when the U-boat submerged. He was unable to come to his aid? He let the man drown.

"In its embryonic stage … and his words these are … the United States is a soft, mouldable entity that will be cast, shaped, if you will, into a national socialist world power. An artist, he says he is … a sculptor! From this country's rough cast, he will chisel a new nation built on the purity, superiority, and rule of the Aryan Race."

"This man understands the influence of ceremony for he held a large assembly … a gathering of German Americans from the Boston area. It was held in a field, just west of Sewell's farm near the Charles River. A thousand or more attended. Curiosity must have brought them there. A speech, he gave, of such power that he was able to recruit a militia of over one hundred and fifty strong men."

"Of what was his speech that would recruit such a number?"

"A summary for you, I will try." He paused a moment. "The United States of America, he said, is founded on principles fabricated with fraudulence and malice and consecrated to God Himself by traitorous Englishmen with parsimonious credentials!"

To Matthew's surprise, the English Captain appeared, by facial expression, to agree with that statement.

"The cultural amalgamate of this nation is a structural impediment where the equality of its people is a manifesto of subjugation, for the freedom of man is but a charade camouflaging a true man's oppression."

"He says that he is the emissary for truth, a harbinger of our future, and a prodigy of intellect and command. He declared himself the prophet of an Aryan God."

Von Friedeburg looked at Matthew.

"He spoke of Canada as a conspicuous aspiration for his need, a trial of his dedication, and a primary illustration of his resolve. His intention is to recruit his militia from Pennsylvania, Kentucky, Massachusetts, New York and Rhode Island. With this militia, he will attack Canada. This strategy, I believe, is but a means to engender favour with Americans, both civilian and soldier alike."

"Of which part of Canada did he speak?" The English Captain made sure Matthew didn't get a chance to ask a question.

Von Friedeburg shrugged. "He spoke of Niagara."

"And how, pray tell, do you come to be here?"

"I was Hartenstein's captive, his slave, made to do his bidding. George, my friend, and the proprietor of my favourite tavern, was also his slave. When he brought his militia to Boston and freed the other sailors from the undersea boat—"

"They have escaped?"

"Freed by Hartenstein, yes. Captain Lawrence was unable to stop him. Now, as to your question, I helped George escape. For that deed, I was beaten and sentenced to death. And dead today, I should be, but I am not without friends."

"If I may, sir, I wish to ask Mister Friedeburg one question?" said Matthew.

"By all means, please do, Mister Brock."

"You spoke earlier of the influence of ceremony. Did this man ... Hartenstein ... make use of any symbols? I'm speaking of signs, banners, salutes, maybe a chant."

"Why yes! He had me build a large cross, shaped much like this." With his finger, von Friedeburg described a swastika in the air. "He also used a straight arm salute ... like so!" Von Friedeburg stood, clicked his heels together, and threw his right arm out in a Nazi salute.

"Did he use a chant?"

"Yes, and very infectious it seemed, for the whole crowd chanted it as they gave the salute!"

"What was this chant?"

Von Friedeburg stiffened, again threw his arm out in the Nazi salute and shouted, loud in the confines of the cabin.

"Hiel Hartenstein!"

CHAPTER 16

▼

The "buzz," as it was referred to in Matthew's navy, a rumour which usually originated from nowhere, word of mouth started by no one, was soon travelling the
length of the berth deck, whispered from hammock to hammock. The watch on
deck sat in small groups on the forecastle and gangway discussing it. The talk
around the wardroom table was animated. The buzz was of adventure in the off-
ing.

Since the invention of sail, every matlot had a favourite spot on board ship. It
was a place of solitude amid the bedlam of shipboard life. Your neighbour may
only be two feet away but you are oblivious to his presence. Physically, you are
crowded; mentally you may be sitting in the shade of an elm, with no one else
around for miles. You can have guests, of course, but they were of your choosing.
Many a young maiden has been compromised under the shade of that elm.

Matthew stood at the port side timberheads, his favourite spot on *Shannon*,
trying to relax. His nerves were tight, and his mind racing. He sat on the butt of a
carronade looking wistfully toward *Blackfoot*. If the buzz was true, he never
thought the opportunity would present itself. He tried to put it from his
thoughts. It may never happen! Besides, there wasn't enough time!

Matthew was sitting in the English Captain's cabin, in what he referred to as
his personal chair. In front of him was the familiar glass of claret. With him was
Ulrich von Friedeburg, included by the English Captain to help, where need be.

"I don't believe Hartenstein will return to the field," said von Friedeburg. "If
he is looking for more recruits, Pennsylvania would be the obvious direction,
there being many German settlements in that state. There is, however, a large

population of German's in New Jersey, and the New York area, to be sure. If I was giving advice to Hartenstein, and I shiver to think of that possibility, I would tell him to travel to New York, before travelling to the Niagara. If it is to Niagara he went, then I would suggest we follow. There are many roads that lead there. Easy travelling, from what I've heard."

"Water is our road, Mister Freideburg," said the English Captain. "If Mister Brock agrees with your assessment, then his ship would be best employed."

"Sir, although I am primarily responsible for the elimination or capture of the undersea boat and crew, I have no power over my captain," said Matthew. "I will put the proposition to him and see what he says."

The English Captain looked from Matthew to von Friedeburg. "First, let me acknowledge that Mister von Friedeburg has a bountiful understanding of Hartenstein, perhaps even how the man thinks. He will accompany you, for he is too valuable an asset to leave behind."

Von Freideburg nodded his head in acknowledgement. "I am most honoured that you think so highly of me. However, I am just an accident of circumstance. In retrospect, it may be most fortunate circumstance, although it was not my thought at the time." He turned to look at Matthew. "I would be most happy to accompany you on this exciting quest. Of course, that is, if you and your captain decide in my favour."

"I have a further request of your captain, Mister Brock." The English Captain took a sip of his claret, and then cleared his throat. "It is my intention to provide, and reasons I have for this resolve, a division of my sailors for your employment." Seeing Matthew's reaction, he held up his hand. "I spoke of reasons, Mister Brock, and I believe you will see the sense of it. To you, citizens of this era are primitive. That makes my point, Mister Brock. A division of your sailors would, and I say this with the utmost respect, arouse suspicion that could put this pursuit in danger of failure." He took another sip of claret, put the glass down, and looked directly at Matthew. "I know of your worry, Mister Brock, however, let me say this. Sailors under my command are the sweepings of streets. Intelligence, they have, I will acknowledge, for conversations that I sometimes overhear on the accommodation deck puts proof to that. Their skills, however, are to cleat a line or holystone the deck. To oversee these sailors, I will provide a midshipman. As you know, a midshipman is a child of higher birth. That, however, doesn't necessarily mean higher intelligence. The lad I have in mind fits that category, for without influence he will not exceed his present position. No danger, do I foresee, of profit being gained by these sailors from your technology. Your mind can rest easy, and your heart will remain pure."

The following forenoon found *Blackfoot* creaming along with what would be described as "a bone in her teeth," steaming south at a speed of twenty-two knots. Her wake, mixed by the spiral of froth generated by the screw, spilled from under her counter, and scribed a straight line on the ocean surface that extended to the horizon. Matthew was back on board as were Ordinary Seamen Bell, Parsons, Booth, and Cripps. They brought with them thirty members of *Shannon's* ship's company, Ulrich von Friedeburg, and one midshipman. The ship's company had volunteered to a man. Even before the word went out for volunteers, British seamen were pestering their petty officers to be given the chance. After morning action stations, the watch below never even climbed back into their hammocks. They stood in large, chatting groups on the forecastle, looking expectantly toward the quarterdeck. Those that were picked were enjoying the delights of a modern destroyer under power.

Ordinary Seamen Booth and Bell were grinning at the group of British tars rather than loading supplies into *Blackfoot's* starboard diesel cutter. "You two … get back to work!" ordered Matthew. "Make sure you record what you stow and where you stow it." He turned his attention to the tars.

"Okay, listen up! Form two ranks along this bulkhead. You will be kitted out … but first; it's a bucket of water and pusser soap for the lot of you. There is much to do and not much time to do it!" He looked aft. "You there, unclasp your eyes from the torpedo tubes and line up!"

The man turned and smiled at Matthew.

"Well, I'll be damned!" Matthew wanted to smile in spite of his anger but he managed to compose his face. The bastard's craftier than he thought.

"Stay where you are, Mister Fulton!" He turned to where Bell and Booth were working. "Ordinary Seaman Bell, escort Mister Fulton to the bridge and introduce him to the Old Man."

Matthew watched them go. Fulton must have bribed a man to let him take his place. Either that or there is one pissed off tar on board the *Shannon*. The English Captain will be pissed off as well, but it is too late now to transfer him back, the *Shannon* being fifty miles astern.

In a little more than two hours the tars were herded naked and "tiddly pink" to the weather deck where the stores department had set up a table stacked high with various sizes of woollen socks, and leather boots. It took another hour of fitting before they resembled well shod sailors. They wore the slops that were issued by *Shannon's* purser, only they had been scrubbed to rid them of vermin. They stood around grinning at each other. Matthew contained his smile when he overheard some of their comments.

"Did yuh cast yer eyes on them heads? Lap o' luxury they are, much better than Cap'n Broke's quarter gallery."

"Aye! I'd be willing to make me mark as a volunteer for this navy. These leather footins pinch a mite, though, an' I'd sooner be without 'em if they'd asked me." The man hefted first his left, then his right foot, looking at each boot.

An able seaman cook passed out mugs, greeted by large, mostly toothless grins of anticipation, which quickly turned to disappointment when a kye barge was produced and thick, steaming hot chocolate was ladled into each mug.

One tar sniffed at his mug. "It could blow a bit more vigorous outta the north." He took a sip. "Bloody 'ell, there ain't no rum in this at all!"

The afternoon was busy, the tars from *Shannon* trained with their muskets. *Blackfoot* left a trail of powder smoke in her wake. The midshipman, who was doing the training, offered a musket to Matthew. "Would you like to try loading and firing one of these?" asked the midshipman.

"I don't know," said Matthew. He'd probably make a fool out of himself in front of the men. Oh well, in for a penny, in for a pound. "Okay … so where do I start?" He took the musket. It was bloody heavy.

The midshipman held up something that looked like a fat cigarette. "This is a cartridge. It contains your powder and ball. It is made of paper and covered with a coating of tallow to make it waterproof." He handed the cartridge to Matthew. "Now, follow my instructions."

"The first thing you do is bite the ball off the end of the cartridge. You keep the ball in your mouth."

Matthew tore the ball off the end. He wasn't going to stick that tallow covered thing in his mouth. He put the ball in his jacket pocket. The midshipman looked at him, his face showing amusement.

"You wouldn't want to do that during a battle, sir. The ball must be kept handy, for a quick access is desired. However, open the pan … it's under the hammer, and pour a small amount of powder into it." Matthew tried to balance the musket, open the pan, and pour in a pinch of powder without spilling any. He acted like a man who needed three hands. He could feel his face turning red.

"That's enough! Now, close the cover and pour the rest of the powder down the barrel."

Matthew's hand was shaking so much that he was spilling a lot of the powder. This was frustrating! The tars thought it funny, barely suppressing their mirth. Matthew glared at them.

"It's best you make a ring around the muzzle with your fist," said the midshipman in a voice meant to calm Matthew. "With your left hand, grip the muzzle so your thumb and forefinger form a ring around it. Aye, that's it."

Matthew succeeded in pouring the rest of the powder down the barrel. He was then told to wad the leftover paper and push it into the barrel, which he did.

"Now, put the ball down the barrel. Most soldiers, in the heat of battle, spit the ball into the barrel. It is much faster." Matthew took the ball from his pocket and put it into the barrel.

"Now with the ramrod, push the ball and wadding down the barrel and tamp it solid." The midshipman watched as Matthew, after two attempts to get the ramrod into the barrel, finally succeeded.

"Good, now replace your ramrod and it's ready to fire." The midshipman looked outboard. "I see some driftwood out there, sir. Let's see if you can hit it."

He noticed that the tars were backing away. The midshipman backed off as well. Not knowing the recoil of a musket, he pulled the musket's butt tightly to his shoulder. He brought the long barrel up and pointed it overboard.

"Don't forget to pull back the hammer, sir," said the midshipman. Matthew glanced at the lad and saw a deadpan look. The boy was hiding his amusement.

He pulled back the hammer, which required some effort due to the stiff spring. Spotting the driftwood, he pointed the musket overboard and aimed along the barrel. Closing his eyes, he pulled the trigger, the hammer released, opening the pan as the flint hit the striker. The powder ignited with flash and smoke. The musket fired, knocking his shoulder back with a violent kick. A cloud of powder smoke blew back into his face.

Lowering the musket, he grinned at the midshipman. "Did I hit my target?"

"I'm sorry, sir. You missed it by a league." The midshipman was barely containing his mirth.

"It's a damn good thing that *Blackfoot's* men will be issued with rifles," thought Matthew.

"What a difference a week makes, eh?" Matthew looked at Ulrich von Friedeburg, who was staring at the electric light bulb that illuminated the small chiefs and petty officer's mess.

Von Friedeburg looked at Matthew, his eyes blinking rapidly.

"So what do you think of our ship?"

"You know, Mister Brock, I'm not an educated man. For you, I'd expect these things"—he flicked a finger at the electric light—"are everyday certainties. That gives you the advantage, I'm afraid, of me."

"No, no! Don't think that!" Matthew realized the man was feeling over-whelmed. "Another person will only have the advantage of you if you allow him."

"I don't understand, for it is into your world that I'm intruding."

"Ahh, but you know, you've got it all wrong. Outside these walls, outside the hull of *Blackfoot*, my world doesn't exist. It's your world out there. A world in your time, and who am I to say that my time is better than yours. You have the advantage of me. I'm locked in here with all these fabulous inventions. If I want to venture outside, I step into your world."

"To be sure, but you have knowledge of all these gadgets and the operation of same. For the love of God, instant light at the pull of a lever, ships that travel at high speed without sails, little boxes that allow you to talk to someone too far away to be seen." Von Friedeburg sat up, getting intense, pointing a finger at Matthew, and stabbing the air. "My good man, how can you say your world is no better than mine?"

Matthew thought for a moment.

"The world is full of opposites, Mister Friedeburg. For day, we have night, for life, we have death. And everything comes with a price. You know, when you want something, you have to pay for it."

Matthew stood, picked up the coffee pot, and poured two mugs of coffee. He placed one on the table in front of von Friedeburg.

"Mankind becomes blinded by his own invention. I hadn't thought about it until I visited your town a few days ago. I've been thinking a lot about it, only I didn't realize it until just now." He sipped his coffee, putting his thoughts in order.

"The thing I noticed most about your time is that no one seems in much of a hurry. You have nothing but time, Mister Friedeburg, and time, you know, is becoming very scarce in my world. Man has become so blinded that he cannot see what is happening to him. These gadgets, as you call them, are taking over, Mister Friedeburg. They are beginning to control man. Of course these gadgets don't let man know that. Men feel they are still in control and just keep on inventing new gadgets. It's becoming a vicious circle where gadgets invent gad-gets."

"As you say, it may be, but your life is easier, is it not?"

"I wish you could see Boston a hundred and twenty years from now. Why, just to cross the street you have to wait until a gadget tells you to. If you don't, you are likely to be run down by someone in a hurry. You start your day being woke up by a gadget, a gadget gets you to work, tells you when to start, when to stop, and when to have lunch. You work harder and longer to make more money to buy more gadgets, which just tell you how, what, and when to do something. It usually only gives you a certain amount of time to do it."

He wasn't sure if von Friedeburg was following him but he didn't know how to better explain it.

"I guess we're all children of our time. I was completely caught up in my world as you are in yours. Perhaps there is a reason for my being here in your time. It is a splash of cold water in the face. You get so wrapped up in your own self-importance that you need to be shocked out of it. Man tends to degrade his history. I would think of your time and say ... I couldn't live like that. Well, now I look at my time and ask myself, how can I live like that?"

He swallowed the remnants of his coffee, stood and stretched. "You know, Mister Friedeburg, I'm not sure that I want to go back to my time."

CHAPTER 17

▼

The following morning, just after zero four hundred hours—one and one half hours before sunrise, *HMCS Blackfoot* anchored, with no lights showing, in Lower Bay, just south of the west end of Coney Island. Her ship's company had been up and active since zero three hundred hours, and by zero five hundred hours, both diesel cutters and the whaler were alongside and manned.

The English Captain wanted *Blackfoot* to return to station off Boston. The Old Man had argued, and rightly so, that *Blackfoot* remain in the New York area to await the return of the expedition as well as conserve fuel. Gardiners Bay at the north end of Long Island was where *Blackfoot* would anchor and remain out of sight. If the expedition hadn't returned by the end of March, *Blackfoot* would proceed to Montreal to rendezvous with them there.

"Oh five hundred, Yeo," said the Jimmy. "You'd better be off. I wish you the best of luck with the mission and God's speed to you and your crew. I wish I was going with you!" The Jimmy glanced at the Old Man who had turned his back. There must have been a heated discussion on the matter.

"Aye-aye, sir, and thank you for the good wishes." Matthew was anxious to get going and could feel his heart pounding. He saluted the Jimmy who returned the salute, signalled Ulrich von Friedeburg to go over the side, turned, checked his beard to make sure his pencil was there, and followed von Friedeburg.

Matthew took charge of *Blackfoot's* starboard cutter. Along with Matthew, aside from von Friedeburg, were Robert Fulton who was to be dropped off in Manhattan, Ordinary Seamen Bell and Booth as watch keepers, and a stoker whose main responsibility was to keep the diesel operating. The diesels were known to become testy when not used often. Huddled under the canopy, are eight of the tars from *Shannon*. Their muskets were wrapped together in a waterproof tarp and lay on the deck at their feet. There wasn't much room for them, the supplies, and other gear. They had no responsibilities in the operation of the cutter, for the time being, they were just along for the ride.

The port side cutter was in the keeping of a killick gunner from X-mount. Along with the killick were Ordinary Seamen Parsons and Cripps acting as seamen watch keepers, a stoker, and eight more tars. Astern of the port side cutter, on a long painter, was the whaler with the remaining members of *Shannon's* ship's company under the command of the midshipman. Most of the supplies for the expedition were stored in the whaler.

"Let go forward!" He watched as Bell unhooked the fall from the bow.

"Slow astern … starboard twenty." The cutter reversed against the stern fall, swinging the bow out from *Blackfoot's* side.

"Let go stern. Slow ahead." Booth unhooked the stern fall and the cutter pulled away from the side, Booth manning the tiller. "Helm amidships!"

Above Matthew, many heads lined *Blackfoot's* rail, watching him go. He could see the Jimmy but the Old Man wasn't there. Astern, the port side cutter was also pulling away. Matthew noted the course on the box compass before tuning to his on-board guest, Robert Fulton, who watched the procedure with no visible emotion, a handkerchief clutched in his left hand.

"You know, Mister Fulton," said Matthew, wanting to seem friendly. "Before tuning in, I took a turn on deck expecting to see the lights of Manhattan reflected in the sky. We must have been close to the north end of Long Island, yet, the sky was dark. The last time I was here, we approached at night as well. Manhattan lit up the southern horizon before we were south of Nantucket Island."

"She develops on a grand scale, I take it."

"New York will become the largest city in the United States, Mister Fulton. In fact, she becomes one of the largest cities in the world. She will be a real cosmopolitan metropolis to be sure."

Fulton smiled. "Hope for the town I have always felt for I have a house here. It seems to me it would be a match between Boston and New York, but from what you say, and you would know, that I should bet on New York for I will profit, to be sure. It is in Philadelphia where my childhood memories take me so as a place of residence, I prefer Philadelphia." Fulton began to cough, bringing his handkerchief to his mouth.

Matthew looked behind, attracted by the clanking of *Blackfoot's* anchor chain as it disappeared into the hawsehole. As soon as the anchor was a'cock bill, *Blackfoot* slowly began making headway.

"I've never seen New York from seaward," said von Friedeburg, getting in on the conversation. "I've only been to the waterfront and from there looked out to sea. Not that there is much to see, of course, only Brooklyn which, on its own, is becoming quite a town ... and Governor's Island, to be sure."

Fulton was looking astern at *Blackfoot*, the ships outline contrasting with the brightening eastern horizon.

The cutter swung north toward The Narrows after rounding Norton Point. Far to port was Staten Island, and close to starboard was Gravesend Bay. Matthew watched the rough, silent, primal beauty as it slipped slowly by. Nature's shoreline, sculptured by century upon century of wind and wave—it looked as if it would stay that way forever. He shook his head, searching his feelings. Facade, that's the word he was looking for. Man builds fugging facades. The harbours of Boston and New York, when he visited them in the thirties, were just facades, shadows of their former beauty. He was lucky to be able to see them in a near virgin state.

"Zero five thirty, Yeoman!"

"Very good, Bell." Matthew looked over his shoulder but was unable to see *Blackfoot*. Astern, the port side cutter was on station. To port, the coast of Staten Island had closed in on them. They were in The Narrows, about five miles from the south tip of Manhattan Island. The foreign sound of the diesel echoed off the bluffs and buildings on both sides, a coughing, hissing, smoking premonition of the next hundred and twenty years. Long Island was fairly flat; a long range of hills ran up its middle like the backbone of a flounder. It seemed to be mostly farmland. Matthew glanced at his chart, barely visible in the weak light. It was a chart from *Shannon*. A chart from *Blackfoot* would be of no use. The landmarks, buoys, shoreline, all would have changed. In fact, Coney Island was, by the forties, part of Long Island. Only a finger of water called Coney Island Creek remained.

Staten Island was higher, the bluffs rising a short distance from the shore. A road was visible along with houses and businesses. They passed a small shipyard along with a number of docks. The facade was already beginning. Staten Island was lined with long piers jutting into The Narrows the last time he was here. At that time, the steam, dirt and odours of merchant ships loading or unloading, the screech of cranes, the rumble and beeps of traffic, the clangs and toots of tugs and ferries, the hustle and bustle of a modern waterfront greeted his eyes and ears.

Matthew navigated to the east of Governor's Island. It was his intention to remain on the Brooklyn side, and then cut directly across to Adam and Noah Brown's shipyard where Fulton wanted to be let off. The port side cutter was to keep to the west of Governor's Island and they were to rendezvous past Manhattan Island at Harlem Creek. They had already separated.

"Where *Blackfoot* is destined, are you party to that knowledge?" The question came out of the blue. Matthew faced Fulton. Obviously the man was testing him, perhaps thinking him trusting.

"Listen, Mister Fulton, if I knew, I wouldn't tell you! I can see right through you, Mister Fulton. I know your motives. You still desire to tour *Blackfoot*."

Fulton looked defiant.

"I also consider you one of the instigators. It is because of you and your fugging gadgets, and men like you with their gadgets, that the world is in one hell of a mess."

Fulton assumed his usual stance, his hands clasped behind his back. "Progress is as the tide, you can not stop it no matter the effort expended to do so."

"Listen, you know, it may be unfair to blame you. Man by nature is inventive. I guess if we weren't, we'd still be swinging from the trees. I have the advantage of you. I can compare my time with your time. I've seen what inventiveness can do if it isn't controlled. I'm for free enterprise and all that, but, please consider the consequences before taking any action."

He made a course correction before continuing.

"I must do the same. If I told you where *Blackfoot* was anchored and somehow you got that tour you want so badly, what would be the consequences of that action?"

Fulton said nothing.

"Well, I'll tell you. Steam technology will suddenly advance by ... let's see ... about eighty-five to ninety years. There would be spin-offs to it. Why, just your knowledge of *Blackfoot's* power train could radically alter the outcome to this war to the detriment of Canada and Britain. I can't allow that!"

"These other ... ah ... spin-offs, as you call them ... just what would those be?" Fulton obviously didn't want to drop the subject. Matthew knew the man was going to try something.

"We're across from the docks. Point out the one where you want to disembark."

Fulton pointed. "Over there. That's the shipyard."

"Very good. That's where we'll drop you off. Cover him, Bell!"

Fulton turned at the sound of a shell sliding into the chamber of a .303 calibre rifle and the "chuck-click" of a bolt being slammed home.

"Sorry, Mister Fulton, but any rash action by you, or any friend on shore who may come to your aid, will not be tolerated."

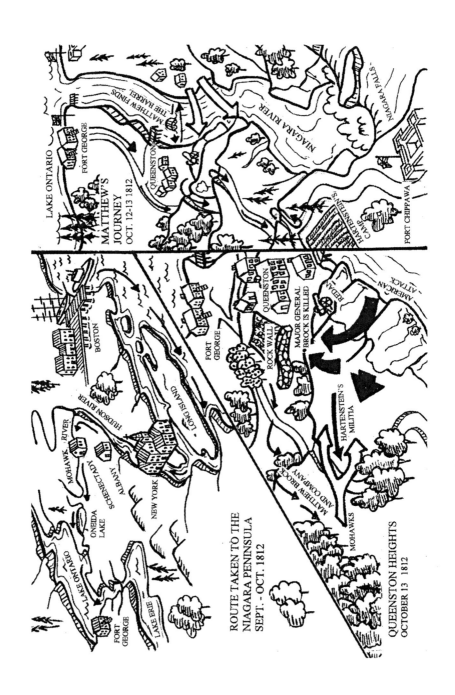

MATTHEW'S
JOURNEY
OCT. 12-13 1812

LAKE ONTARIO

FORT GEORGE

MATTHEW FINDS
THE BARREL

QUEENSTON

NIAGARA RIVER

NIAGARA FALLS

HARTENSTEIN'S CAMP

FORT CHIPPAWA

ROUTE TAKEN TO THE
NIAGARA PENINSULA
SEPT. - OCT. 1812

BOSTON

HUDSON RIVER

MOHAWK RIVER

ONEIDA LAKE

SCHENECTADY

ALBANY

NEW YORK

LONG ISLAND

LAKE ONTARIO

FORT GEORGE

LAKE ERIE

FORT GEORGE

QUEENSTON

ROCK WALL

MAJOR GENERAL
BROCK IS KILLED

REDAN

AMERICAN
ATTACK

HARTENSTEIN'S
MILITIA

MATTHEW BROCK
AND COMPANY

MOHAWKS

QUEENSTON HEIGHTS
OCTOBER 13 1812

CHAPTER 18

▼

When the sun rose that morning, Matthew and crew were north of Paulus Hook. To starboard the town of New York was just waking up. Matthew hoped that by staying close to the Jersey shore of the Hudson River, his boat would be less noticeable against the dark shoreline. Luckily, there had been no ships at anchor in Upper Bay or in the harbour proper. The flood tide and light breeze prevented any ships from leaving. The rendezvous with the other cutter was still ahead.

On the Manhattan side of the Hudson, buildings, mostly brick warehouses standing three to four stories, lined the waterfront. Each floor had a large doorway that opened to admit the cargoes that were embarked from the traders that lined the jetties. A block and tackle arrangement, jutting over the jetty, could be seen attached to a roof centre-beam of each warehouse. Further up river, the warehouses thinned, the buildings became lower. By the time they had travelled three miles, the buildings lining the shore were mostly dwellings, giving way to meadows and orchards.

The New Jersey side was flat, mostly farmland. Small boats sat at docks to be used as transportation to the town—for supplies, taking children to school, or perhaps work.

Thoughts of Fulton still bothered Matthew and he had to get them out of his system.

"I am very surprised, you know, that the Old Man promised to drop Fulton off where he wanted to go. Shit, I'd have rowed him to the nearest shore and left him there."

"Mister Fulton is a gentleman and as such should not be treated in a callous manner." Von Friedeburg seemed offended by the idea. "Perhaps you may be right … for your time, but … you may blow a fellow's brains out in my time, however, you still do it in a gentlemanly manner. Pistols at dawn, a ten pace walk, a slow turn, take careful aim, and fire. That's it! If survive you do … a gentleman you are … if not … well, at least you were killed in a gentlemanly manner. It is the same on the battlefield. You stand upright in rank and file, ready to receive as you give out."

"You are a soldier, Mister Friedeburg?"

"Yes, I was a soldier … a Hessian!"

"Then you fought alongside the British. What did you think of the American style of fighting? You know, compared to Europe."

"The American manner of fighting astonished me. At first, I believed the Americans to be unworthy of being called soldiers. They fought like the native Indian, firing from behind trees and stone fences. My comrades and I marched, manoeuvred, and fired in the open. At the very least, the Americans could have shown themselves as equal targets."

"Well, gentleman or not, I still would have thrown Fulton ashore. From what you heard and told us, it was his fault that this Hartenstein bastard escaped by trying to get a tour of the U-boat. It is because of him that we now have to embark on this Lewis-and-Clarke expedition through the wilds of New England."

At 0900 hours, at the spot where Manhattan became an island, where Harlem Creek created a channel from the Hudson to the East river, they rendezvoused with the port side cutter. Above them was the crumbling fort built by the Dutch named Spuyten Duyvil. It was last used in defence of the Hudson against probing British warships in 1776. The fort was overgrown with deciduous trees and underbrush, a few of its parapets were visible, grey and moss covered, streaked with the decay of neglect.

The New Jersey shoreline became steep. High palisades of rock jutted vertically from the alluvial till which angled sharply upward from the river's bank. Hardy, spindly pines clung tenaciously to the rocks.

"My memories are astir in all their horror." Ulrich von Friedeburg leaned heavily on the forward canopy, stretching his neck to look at the heights. Small drops of sweat dotted his forehead and chin.

"You've been here before?"

"Jah!" Von Friedeburg drew a handkerchief from his pocket and mopped his chin and brow. "I've been thinking all morning of my time here in seventy-six. It was George Washington we had on the run when we Hessians landed below Brooklyn. We chased him as a hound would a rabbit after inflicting grievous damage to his army. High-tail it, they did, crossing the East River to Manhattan Island and retreating to Harlem Creek here, where they encamped, and fortified their position. If I remember correctly, that was August. Howe, in his wisdom, sent some of his warships up river and they were knocked about by that fort over there and a battery opposite on the cliff."

He pointed at the cliff. "Scale that, we did, after Washington crossed to this side. My bones still ache from hauling those bloody field pieces up these cliffs. However ... it was all for naught as Washington took his revenge of us on Christmas Day at Trenton. It weren't too long after that I deserted."

"Why did you desert?"

"The way a certain lady kicked her petty coats caused me great distraction."

"I see," said Matthew. His back teeth were floating. He stood on the canopy, balanced himself, undid his fly and had a satisfying leak as he surveyed the heights above him. Von Friedeburg, Bell and Booth, all suddenly had things on the opposite side of the river that occupied their attention.

The road between Albany and Schenectady was well travelled and quite easy going. The New England autumn was spectacular in its brilliance, the noon sun shafted through a mixed forest. Tall, straight birches lined the road, their black and white bark playing hide and seek with the shadows of leaves and branches of spreading oaks. The colours of fall, scarlet, crimson and yellow were back-dropped by tall pine and hemlock. Alternate patches of dark greens and bright colours covered the Catskill Mountains to the south and west, and the Adirondack Mountains to the north. Matthew could care less. He had a long walk ahead of him and he didn't relish the thought of it.

The trip up river to Albany only took a day and a half, the river being tidal and easily navigable that far north. Above Albany it became a raging torrent, filled with rapids and many waterfalls. A lot of goods that flowed down river to New York were manufactured or ground in the mills that made use of the river's energy. They'd passed a number of barges laden with goods heading down river using oar, wind and tide. At the sight of the two diesel cutters coughing their way up river, two or three individuals actually fell overboard. A barge, under oars, was hurriedly rowed to the opposite bank and run aground, the crew disappearing into the underbrush. Another, under sail, suffered a broken boom when it accidentally gibed, an accompanying freighter canoe overturned, dumping men and cargo into the cold water.

They passed one steam vessel heading down river towards New York. It looked to be well over a hundred feet in length with a wedge shaped bow and stern. It had a bowsprit and two masts with accommodation for sails. It had a poop deck and a quarterdeck with a large awning spread over it. Two enormous paddle wheels were mounted directly abeam, one each side of the large engine. The boiler with its single stack was mounted in brickwork aft of the engine. There was a small crowd of passengers lining the rail on deck, losing interest in the steam vessel and paying attention to the two diesel cutters heading up river. As the steam vessel passed astern, its name could be seen on its transom. Her name was *Clermont*.

Soon after they landed, Von Friedeburg had gone ahead to Schenectady to arrange for suitable vessels, along with a wagon with a team of horses to carry them, so they could continue their journey along the Mohawk River which flowed into the Hudson about ten miles up river from Albany. Matthew had the whaler and cutters unloaded of supplies, which were packed and made ready for carrying overland. This was in a secluded bay a few miles down river from the road to the town. A small peninsula of rock and willow created a tidal backwater where they could safely work unnoticed. The boats were hidden amongst the trees and covered with bushes. Matthew hoped the cover was adequate because if the boats were lost, then so was he and the rest of his crew.

Matthew felt nervous as night fell. He didn't know if it was the fact that the wilderness took on an ominous personality or if it was a premonition of some kind—some future disaster. He stopped at a short wooden bridge that crossed a creek and told his men to rest, and if needed, fill their canteens.

He searched the gloom ahead where the road took a bend to the left. Above the tree line, the stars seemed to dance and shimmer. The tops of the trees were reflecting first orange, then yellow, then red. Matthew spoke to the killick gunner.

"Keep the men here, they need a rest. I'm going on ahead. Follow me in thirty minutes. I'll be waiting for you."

Reaching the corner he stopped and listened. He could hear cracks and pops of a large fire; its heat had caused the stars to dance. He slipped a magazine into his .303 and chambered a shell. He moved ahead, now more cautious, making sure he didn't stumble or kick a stone. Ahead the road took a bend to the right. The fire reflected off the trees on the left, the fire being on the right, hidden by the corner. The tree line stopped at the bend, giving way to a snake rail fence, the rails showing white and pink in the light of the flames.

Seeing no one, Matthew approached the corner with care, afraid of what he would see and he paled when he saw it. The fire, the burning remnants of a farm—the house and barn being reduced to ashes—cast its appalling light in a wide circle. There, to the left of the burning barn, a man's body was bound to a tree, head hanging, tongue lolling, his chest a bloody pulp. The man had been executed.

He approached the body and lifted the head. It wasn't von Friedeburg! Matthew didn't recognize the man. Who was he and why was he shot? He had a feeling it was Hartenstein's doing. He can't be far ahead. His hands felt hot!

Thirty minutes later, when his company arrived on the scene, they gave the man a decent burial. Matthew paced as the burial took place, pondering the fate of von Friedeburg. He looked up as Ordinary Seaman Booth approached him. "What is it, Booth?"

"Sorry Chief," said Booth, looking down in the mouth. "My rifle seems to be missing."

CHAPTER 19

─────────── ▼ ───────────

It took five days to travel the hundred miles up the Mohawk River valley from Schenectady to Rome and the mile long portage that led to Wood Creek. It was fairly good road for the most part, passing through forest and farmland. Matthew was able to hire a horse, wagon, and driver to haul the heavy canoes and supplies, arrangements that were made by von Friedeburg. It took a full day to pack the freight canoes, supplies and ammunition along the portage which had been used by Amherst when he, Haviland and Murray led their English forces by three separate routes to attack Montreal in 1760. It took two more days, fighting swift water, overhanging branches, beaver dams, and shallows of Wood Creek, to make the easy waters of Oneida Lake. It was at its outfall, the beginning of the Oswego River, that they finally rested.

Matthew grew up in the city, and as a child, aside from the two camping trips to the Fraser Valley and the occasional trip to the North Shore with his father, the streets, buildings and back alleys of Vancouver comprised the only landscape he knew. The forest his father took him to was enticing, and under the protection of his father, very friendly. Here, in the backwoods and on the frontier trails of 1812 New England, Matthew slowly came to an understanding of the dichotomy of the natural world. Sure, wilderness can be your friend, but it can also be your enemy. At times it welcomes you, shows you the way, feeds and cloths you; at times it throws obstacles in your path, barricades that make you accommodate, change direction, and subjugate yourself. It can dazzle you by its brilliance, it can enrich you with its abundance, and it can perplex you with extremes. The wilderness has dominion over your actions, thoughts, and bodily functions. He thought back to his conversation with von Friedeburg. Modern man with his cities has created his own wilderness, only abstracted by man's supposed intellect.

The men under his command saw wilderness as an enemy and they cursed it. They shouted obscenities at the water for its falls and rapids. They yelled malediction at the warm sun for its sweat. They snarled imprecation at the rain for its cold and discomfort. They complained vociferously about the underbrush, the thorns, and the windfalls that blocked their way. They blasphemed through chattering teeth at the cold of the night.

Years of exposure to the sanded planking of a Royal Navy frigate can harden the soles of your feet into callused leather. One week of exposure to the hardness of modern naval footwear can chafe your feet into bleeding scrapes and blisters. Bodies used to expending rapid amounts of energy between long periods of rest, capitulated to the utilization of extremities for extended periods. In other words, it was a damned hard slog.

Von Friedeburg was nowhere to be seen. He made the arrangements at Schenectady, as was his assignment, but then he left, leaving behind a note with a merchant saying he had a score to settle with Hartenstein.

Matthew had no way of telling if Hartenstein was only one or two days ahead, that is, if he was heading for the Niagara. He could have headed toward Montreal via Lake Champlain. Questions asked of residents of Rome were met with blank stares or intentional avoidance. The trail was littered with campsites, some fresh, and some old. There could be another group of men ahead of them on the trail but there was nothing that pointed to Hartenstein.

Urgency necessitated that the expedition stay at Lake Oneida only one day for a much needed rest. It was raining heavily when they left, the clouds hung low between the surrounding hills, and a wind whipped the lake into white caps. The Oswego River meandered through low hills, sweeping northwest for five miles before turning back on itself and retreating to the southeast for five miles. The river didn't advance in a constant compass heading until they were below where the Seneca River flowed in from the south. It took four and a half days from Lake Oneida to reach the south shore of Lake Ontario, after having to portage around Oswego Falls. They passed the town of Oswego in the twilight of evening so as not to attract undue attention. The lights of town looked inviting and from what Matthew could see, there was not one amongst his troop that didn't cast a longing look at the warm houses along the shore. That included Matthew.

At the mouth of the river, high on an escarpment on the east side, stood the American fort. The Americans wouldn't be watching for the enemy to come from their territory and paid them no attention. They turned west-southwest directly into a belting breeze. The men in the bows were soaked in spite of their oilskins. The year was now into its tenth month, the wind foretelling the approaching winter season. They camped that night five miles from Oswego, huddling under sheltering evergreens or under the overturned canoes.

Staying close to shore, ducking into hiding at the sight of other lake traffic, they managed fifteen miles a day. On the evening of October tenth, they approached Fort George on the Canadian side of the Niagara River. The scene was almost biblical. When the river and the naval yard at Newark came in sight, the overcast to the west opened to allow shafts from the setting sun to highlight the scene in contrasts of light and shadow. The fort with its two story block-houses was a short distance up river. The American fort, an older one built by the French, stood across the river, not more than one cable's distance from the naval docks.

He had made it! No, they had made it! They rested on their paddles that they placed across the thwarts, allowing the canoes to glide as they gazed at the scene. The hunt for Hartenstein could now begin in earnest.

The trials of pioneer travel had relegated thoughts of his great great uncle to his subconscious mind. Now, as he looked forward to the welcome ahead, a suppressed realization leapt to the forefront of his mind that immediately tensed his muscles, his mind unable to grapple the enormity of it. Just ahead, in one of those buildings, sits his long dead great uncle. Oh God! What can he say to him? How can he prove who he is?

Major General Isaac Brock placed his quill in the ink well and blew upon the paper to dry the ink. He held the paper up to a beam of sunlight that lanced over his left shoulder from the one small, paned window behind his desk. He smiled, folded the paper and sealed it with wax. He passed the folded paper to his aide, brushed some dust from the desk, placed his hands flat in front of him and looked directly into Matthew's eyes. Matthew was standing at attention, trying hard not to shake, cap in hand by his right leg. Did he see a flicker of recognition there? No—it couldn't be—it's not possible!

This was the moment Matthew looked forward to. He had stood on the deck of *Shannon* and reached out with his heart and embraced the hope that this moment would happen, although he knew it was beyond any realm of possibility. It was also the moment he dreaded, unable to sleep the previous night in spite of his fatigue, first sweating, then feeling chilled, his mind going a mile a minute. He knew it was nerves, but try telling his brain that. His bloody brain just wouldn't listen! He tried meeting his uncle's eyes, but kept looking away. He had to concentrate, meet his eyes, and show confidence in spite of the fact that his bowels were water. God, his hands started to shake. This meeting—it's fugging impossible! He can't be here. This can't be him. This can't be happening!

What could he say? What do you say to a dead ancestor? Especially when your image of that ancestor is preconceived, and that preconception is based on positive, glowing reports in textbooks and family word of mouth. Through the filter of history, the negative aspects of a personality would tend to disappear. What if his uncle was a loud, rude, obnoxious drunk that yelled obscenities and farted and belched profusely? Preconceptions quickly disappear when faced with the real man.

"Who ... or what ... may I ask, are you?"

Shit! Should he tell him? No, better not, at least not yet! Christ, his heart was pounding!

"I ... I ... represent His Majesty's Canadian Ship *Blackfoot.*" He was sweating; he could feel it running down his forehead and into his eyebrows.

His uncle didn't change expression. He sat back in his chair and just stared at him, eyes squinting. Does he recognize Matthew as family? There is something there—in his eyes.

"Kindly remove yourself from my presence for much too busy I am for crackpots." His uncle waved his hand in dismissal.

"But ... but, I have something to show you, sir."

Although his facial expression never changed except for a muscle that jumped in his right cheek, his uncle's eyes expressed anger. He called for his aide who immediately entered the room. "Escort this man from my presence."

Matthew, concentrating on keeping his hand from shaking, reached under his tunic and pulled out a Browning 9mm pistol and displayed it as a magician would display his trick hat. He had mentally rehearsed this performance and now that he was into it, he felt calmer, and in control. He quickly pulled back the cocking mechanism, pointed the pistol at a large log in the wall and pumped five slugs into it in rapid succession. The shots inside the small room were deafening. His uncle's aide placed his hands over his ears and showed signs of panic. His uncle showed no reaction.

Matthew popped the clip with its remaining shells from the pistol's handle, reached over and laid the pistol in front of his uncle, its barrel smoking. He thumbed a bullet from the magazine and placed it on end beside the pistol.

"I realize that I am quite out of line and I apologize for the boldness of this demonstration, sir, but I felt it to be the only way to get you to give me an audience."

His uncle waved his aide away. "It's all right, I thank you, John." He reached out and touched the pistol. He looked at Matthew.

"Are you a salesman?"

"No, sir. I'm a Warrant Officer in the Royal Canadian Navy."

"If a Canadian Navy there was, I would be the first to know about it. I will ask you one more time. Who are you? And what do you want from me?"

"If you look closely at the pistol, sir, you will see its make and year of manufacture engraved on the barrel. It may explain my situation faster than I can."

His uncle picked up the pistol and held it to the beam of sunlight, squinting to see the engraving. His head snapped around to look at Matthew before slowly returning to stare again at the pistol. He placed the pistol on the desk and saying nothing, pulled open a drawer and took out a small folded paper. He unfolded this and placed it on his desk before looking at Matthew.

"Mister Matthew Isaac Brock ... do you know this man?"

God! Now Matthew really had to go to the head—bad! It was his note, the note he'd written in Boston and entrusted to Robert Fulton! Matthew didn't answer. He couldn't. His mind wouldn't let him.

"A few days ago this note arrived, it came overland from Boston. Except for strange circumstance, I would have dismissed it as from a crank and torn it up." He looked at Matthew again, his eyes, could he know? He indicated a chair. "Here, be seated, for you look to have journeyed far."

"Err ... thank you, sir." Matthew sat down. The chair was comfortable, relaxing, for his tension returned with the production of his note. He swallowed. "May I ask of the strange circumstance?"

His uncle adjusted the yellow sash that crossed his chest from his left shoulder to his right hip. He then tugged each cuff to cover his wrists, his eyes looking at the ceiling as if trying to recall the day.

"I was in conference with Tecumseh, the Indian leader, when the note arrived. Tecumseh's brother, Lolawauchika, was in the room but not taking part in the conversation. It was with disgust I read this note and was about to crumple it when Lolawauchika seized it from my hand. Have you ever met this Indian?"

"No, sir. I have heard of Tecumseh, though." Yeah, sure, in history books!

"Well, it's not important. Anyway, to continue, he hopped about this room waving the note in a manner I would describe as frantic, and talking in a tongue I've never heard."

His uncle seemed to wilt. His eyes glistened when he looked at Matthew. He knows!

"Amongst his people, Lolawauchika is well known as having the gift, an ability, it seems, to predict the future. His people call him The Prophet." His uncle picked up the note. "This note came from this world, he told me, but not from this time. It comes from the world where men exist before life. The writer of this note is not yet born!"

He sat quietly, for just a moment, placing the note back on his desk. "The Prophet also told me that this note was written by an unborn descendant of my family but not of my loins." He looked at Matthew, his eyes now betraying sureness. "Perhaps, sir, more to this there is, and you can enlighten me, if you so please."

Matthew sat up. It's now or never as his Mother used to say.

"I am ... and perhaps you already have guessed this ... I am Matthew Isaac Brock, your great great nephew!"

CHAPTER 20

▼

"Sir, you spoke earlier of strange circumstance. You could call it accident, or fluke … maybe even destiny. Your Indian friend is correct … and most likely is a prophet!"

His uncle reached into a pocket and pulled out a small tin. Matthew continued.

"Though I sit here in front of you today a grown man, I have not yet been born."

Opening the small tin, his uncle placed a pinch of snuff on the back of his right wrist. Matthew continued, although he began to wonder if his uncle was listening.

"My being here is the result of an idiosyncrasy, a loss of symmetry, if you will, of the measure of sequential occurrence where second follows second, minute follows minute, hour follows hour and so forth."

Plugging one nostril with a finger, his uncle snorted a quantity of snuff. Plugging the other, he snorted the rest. Matthew decided he'd better wait till his uncle finished.

His uncle started blinking rapidly, his eyes began to water. He pulled a handkerchief from his sleeve to cover his mouth. Squeezing his eyes together, he lay his head back and let go a gigantic sneeze, violently throwing his head forward. Blowing his nose, he nodded to Matthew. "Most interesting, please continue."

"Yes, sir. Thank you." Matthew took a deep breath while he collected his thoughts—he'd been on a roll. "Contemporary epochs, mine and yours, both have their devils. These villains remain within their period of history, leaving their impression upon that era and its peoples, the actions and events of their cause work themselves out with the passage of time, some have effect for centuries. Your devil is Napoleon."

His uncle nodded his understanding. He reached in front of him to pick up and examine the bullet Matthew had placed there. He looked at Matthew to show he was listening.

"It is absurd to suggest that even one hour be effected by an hour not yet come. It is doubly absurd to think that one era would be effected by the happenings of a coming era, one that is separated by the buffer of a hundred years. But … I'm afraid that's what has happened!"

Matthew saw his uncle's eyes widen.

"In short, as a result of the same circumstance that finds me here, the devil of my time is loose and running amuck in yours. If allowed, the hell he could create for Canada as well as the United States will make the next hundred years unliveable. If he is allowed to carry out his ambitious plan, there will be no Canada, no United States. I may never be born. This man and his evil must be stopped before he gets too big. I'm not sure how many men he has under his command; the last I heard was about one hundred and fifty. It may be a small number, but small usually gets bigger. It's nature's way. That is what brings me here to this place, on this day. He is also someplace here. I must find and destroy him. In my time, because the world didn't act as it should have, we are locked in conflict to stop his kind. That conflict must not cease."

His uncle sat quietly for a moment, as if trying to sort out what Matthew was saying. He smiled for the first time. "If you please … perhaps it would be best if you start at the beginning. I want all the details … leave nothing out."

"Well, sir, the beginning …" When was the beginning? "I guess this whole thing started in September of the year nineteen forty one …"

"Your duties at Queenston aside, a third request I have of you, and this is just between us." Matthew's uncle was escorting Brigade Major Thomas Evans to the door of his office. Matthew quickly retrieved the pistol off the general's desk before following. They came to a halt at the door.

"After consulting Major General van Rensselaer regarding prisoner exchange, I want you to ask some questions of the general. Determine, if you can, knowledge he may have of a German militia from Massachusetts. This information is very important to Mister Brock and his platoon."

Major Evans looked at Matthew, his lips firmed in a straight line. No doubt he was wondering who Matthew was and what he was doing in the general's office. "I understand, sir. Regarding Mister Brock … should I place him under my command?"

"As I was about to explain, Mister Brock is detached under orders of Captain Broke of His Britannic Majesty's Ship *Shannon*. He and his men are to remain apart from our forces. However … Mister Brock knows what and who to look for. It is he who can identify the leader of the German militia. I believe it best that Mister Brock and his men accompany you … under your temporary command … to Queenston. Mister Brock will accompany you to the American side. After that, you may make use of Mister Brock, and his men if needed, otherwise they are to be kept separate."

"I see, sir!"

Matthew's uncle turned back to his desk. Major Evans must have taken that as a dismissal as he made to leave. Matthew followed, leaving his great great uncle, perhaps to history's record, not knowing if he would see him again. Funny! His uncle never asked any questions of family—nothing! The whole meeting was impersonal, kept that way by his uncle. Well, perhaps it is best! No! He wanted to help him—save him from his early death. His uncle must know his reward.

It was the first time Matthew was under fire. The Americans were sniping at the soldiers in Queenston from across the Niagara River, and from what Matthew heard, had been doing so for a couple of days. He and Major Evans were being shot at as they rowed across the Niagara in spite of the white flag on a staff at the bow of their boat. Matthew was beginning to get a little worried.

"Don't dwell on it," said Evans who must have noted his distress. "A musket that is aimed will usually never hit its target … for accurate, they are not. If you are wounded or killed, accident rather than skill is the cause."

"Why … thank you, sir, most comforting." Matthew, thinking maybe that he was a bit too sarcastic, crouched lower over his paddle, a musket ball buzzing past his ear.

As they neared the American side, the musket fire stopped. The Americans even helped them ashore. They went in search of an officer.

"Look, Mister Brock," whispered Evans. "They have hidden boats in crevices … there … along the river!"

"I see them, sir. You can take it from me, they will attack, and soon!" Matthew was still unsure of the date, originally thinking that the battle of Queenston Heights had taken place in September, and that he would be too late to help his great great uncle. Now he didn't know if he'd see him again in time to help!

While Evans met with his American counterpart to discuss prisoner exchange, Matthew looked for signs of Hartenstein and his mob. His questions about a German militia from Massachusetts were scoffed at. Massachusetts didn't support the war, even refusing to send a militia. As for Germans, there were some in every militia. Matthew was unable to secure any information.

Evans was anxious to get back and alert the troops in Queenston and warn Matthew's uncle of the impending attack. They began their return journey, Matthew feeling unsure of where to go from there. Maybe Hartenstein hadn't arrived. Maybe he hadn't planned to be here. He may have sent them on a merry chase while he ravaged another part of the country.

"What's that?" Major Evans pointed up river.

Matthew squinted. "Looks like a barrel, sir!"

"Yes, yes, now I can see it is."

They continued rowing as they watched the barrel come towards them. It was low in the water and not affected by the small waves that rocked their boat.

Matthew studied the barrel. "Sir, I see a human hand! Someone must be in the barrel!"

Seeing that the barrel would pass behind them if they continued as they were, they changed course to intercept it.

"It is badly damaged," said Evans as they approached. "You are correct! It is not possible, but this barrel contains a man!"

Through a jagged hole in the top of the barrel, a man's ear could be seen. The hand that protruded was lacerated, the blood washed away by the river.

Further investigation was impossible without the barrel being on shore. They resumed their original course, Matthew paddling as the major, with great difficulty, dragged the barrel, gripping it by the hole in its top.

Major Evans called for help and the barrel was dragged ashore and set on its side behind a stone fence. By some miracle the barrel hadn't sunk, as a number of staves were broken. An iron bar was found and it was used to pry off the top. By reaching inside, Matthew dragged the sodden corpse from the barrel.

"Well, I'll be damned." Matthew stood up and wiped his forehead, oblivious to the musket balls that passed near him. He stared at the cut, bruised face of the dead man.

"Do you know him?"

"The man's name is Ulrich von Friedeburg. He was our guide through the wilderness. He went missing at Schenectady after leaving behind a note saying he had a personal score to settle with the leader of the German Militia." Matthew looked up river as the realization dawned on him—Hartenstein was here! His cold hands suddenly felt hot! "I guess he found them and it looks like they settled the score."

He looked back at Friedeburg, a thought suddenly coming to mind. Funny how in times of distress when you think you need control, the mind takes its own path, going places which surprise you. He again looked up river.

"Yes, Mister Friedeburg," he said out loud, "It looks like you're the first man over Niagara Falls in a barrel, and it's a pity my friend, that your name will never be mentioned in history books."

Tears flowed freely down his cheeks and into his beard as he bent down and tried closing the corpse's eyes. Major Evans, who had left without Matthew noticing, returned with a blanket and covered the body—the body of a fat man who had a big sense of what was right and what was wrong. Von Friedeburg died for what was right.

CHAPTER 21

▼

Matthew followed Queenston's main street as it climbed to the heights south of the village, passing a gun position that overlooked the river, and the American town of Lewiston on the opposite bank. Where the main street intersected the road, which he suspected led to Niagara Falls; he paused and looked back at the scene spread before him.

He was alone; leaving his men camped in an orchard behind the protective walls of a deserted house. His intention was to find Hartenstein and his militia and scout their location, before bringing his men into action. He would need the help of Major Evans, of course. His few men couldn't handle a militia the size of Hartenstein's. He intended to walk as far as Fort Erie on the Canadian side and if he didn't come in contact with Hartenstein, he would cross to Black Rock on the American side and make his way back down stream. It was at least thirty miles to Fort Erie and even farther to make his way back on the New York side. As he stood on the escarpment overlooking Queenston, he began to question his motives, which had perhaps been influenced to the point of irresponsibility by the finding of Ulrich von Friedeburg.

Below him the village of Queenston consisted of approximately twenty spaced houses surrounded by orchards and small gardens. Soon, very soon, the village and the heights where he stood would be filled with men locked in a life and death struggle. American regulars and militia against British regulars and Canadian militia—along with Mohawks, a tribe whose fighting skills and ferocious deportment struck fear into the hearts of all who faced them on the field of battle. Close to where he stood, his great great uncle, Major General Isaac Brock, would die. Here, on these heights, a tall column would be raised and an effigy of his

famous uncle would look down upon the tourist families and honeymoon cou-
ples that would pass on their way to the falls. Small faces would turn to look up at
him with questioning eyes. Small arms would tug at the skirts of mothers who
would barely give him a second glance. Questions, in small voices, would be
asked about him. Hurried parents would consult gate folded glossy brochures
that contain a three-line acknowledgment of his accomplishments. These would
be quickly read and the child dragged along by the parent, the small face looking
back and up at him, still full of questions that wouldn't be answered.

It was an easy road to walk, carpeted with a mattress of wet, fallen leaves, the
majority a golden yellow in colour. He walked at least six miles without stopping,
something he couldn't have done before he'd embarked on this pursuit of
Hartenstein. It was dark by the time he could hear the roar of the falls.

The road followed the escarpment that had been carved as the falls slowly,
through millennia, eroded its way up river. A fog was rolling down river in waves,
urged on by the draft of the falls. The clouds built as darkness fell and now sleet,
a mixture of snow and rain that his mother used to call "snain," was beginning to
fall. Matthew picked up his pace, beginning to wonder about his reception at
Fort Chippawa.

He was approaching an intersection where a road branched off to the west.
Before he got to it, he could see the glow of a large fire reflecting through a curtain of fog that formed along the branch road. There was no sound other than the
roar of the falls. He stopped.

He'd seen it as a youngster, a skit that took place on a stage behind a white
curtain, the characters backlit, throwing their shadows onto the curtain. It was
usually a medical skit—an abdominal operation. A carpenter's saw was used to
imitate a scalpel; a long string of sausages would be used to mimic intestines.

This skit had the shadow of only one character that was backlit by the fire and
cast upon the curtain of fog. His movements reminded Matthew of Charlie
Chaplain, overly dramatic and jerky. The shadow strutted and stomped, throwing its arms about. Matthew watched the comic display, unable to suppress a
smile. His expression changed when the shadow came to rigid attention, shooting
an arm out at forty-five degrees from vertical. The shadow was giving the Nazi
salute. Holy shit! It was Hartenstein!

Matthew's hands became hot, gripping his rifle so hard his knuckles turned
white. Without thinking about it, he brought the rifle to the high-port position,
drew back the bolt and slid a shell into the chamber from the magazine. Slowly
he brought his rifle to eye level and looking beyond at the prancing shadow, he

brought the bead of the fore sight into the notch of the rear sight while he felt for the trigger.

His demon was making itself known; its life force surging to his extremities in wave after powerful wave. His hands and feet tingled; his ears glowed with warmth, his mind was a battlefield where his classic good was in contention with his internal evil for control over his mind and soul. His eyes narrowed, losing peripheral vision, his total concentration focused on his target. An energy from within surged along the barrel to illuminate the bead of the fore sight to diamond intensity. His breath turned warm, his chest surging—but his demon was groggy, not yet fully awake for it had been a long sleep, a hibernation that lasted the span of a thousand empires. The rational thinking Matthew was not about to submit or even declare a truce and the battle was hard fought, his finger tightening, and then lessening pressure on the trigger as one or the other gained dominance.

His demon was now fully awake and it spoke with an atrocious voice that seemed to echo through the ages of man. His demon urged Matthew to take immediate and violent action, its hot, putrid breath momentarily driving back its opponent.

The judicious side of Matthew boldly stepped forward to urge consideration before hostility, stating that it would be foolish to shoot at a shadow. There are problems with distortion and refraction. The target could be to the left or the right of the shadow.

Common sense prevailed, his demon seeing defeat, tactfully withdrew back to its hidden den. Literally shaking from his internal struggle, Matthew lowered his rifle, and almost tripping as he turned, stumbled onto the road back to Queenston. He could feel the panic; the undeniable need to get the hell out of there. He forced himself to walk, looking over his shoulder at the fog curtain and glow of the fire. He had located his game, now he had to get back and inform his hunting party.

The sleet was falling harder, blowing directly into his face, soaking his beard and dripping down his collar that he'd turned up against the cold. The leaves which he originally saw as a soft carpet were now slippery, making footing difficult in places. The noise created by the falls slowly receded behind him only to be replaced by another noise in front of him, the sound of cannon fire. That could only mean one thing; the battle for Queenston Heights had begun. He didn't know what time it was; only that it was well past midnight. He picked up his pace.

The sky had lightened through the overcast when he came to the edge of the woods on Queenston Heights. He stopped to survey the situation before proceeding. The heights were clear except for a squad of redcoats.

Putting his rifle to the high port he started off at the double, heading for the gun emplacement at the top of the escarpment, just south of the village. As he ran he saw his great great uncle, resplendent in his bright scarlet coat and plumed hat, ride up to the squad of redcoats and talk to them. He then turned his horse and disappeared over the edge of the escarpment. It was toward that spot that Matthew ran.

A passing musket ball forced him to the ground. He looked to his right. Men, led by a young looking officer who limped, appeared over the lip of the river's steep embankment. Two of them broke away and with levelled bayonets, ran toward Matthew. Scrambling to his feet and making sure he hung onto his rifle, he ran flat out for the gun emplacement. He leapt over the edge of the escarpment and tumbled head over heels before sliding to a stop, creating an avalanche of small stones.

His great great uncle looked his way and then, mouth open, at the top of the escarpment where screaming, running Americans were charging. His reaction was swift, directing a gunner to jam his ramrod into the touchhole of the eighteen-pound cannon before ordering a retreat down hill. Matthew got to his feet, picked up his rifle, and stumbled after them. He took refuge behind a wall of stone at the base of the hill. He was out of breath and dizzy from his tumble.

He could hear his uncle speaking to soldiers, organizing them for a frontal attack. "Take a moment to regain your breath, for to win this day all your energy will be required." He looked and saw that his uncle had dismounted and was walking towards him. His uncle sat beside him and looked him in the eye.

"It is time for my death, is it not?" His uncle said it more as a statement than a question. His voice was calm.

"Not if I can help it!" Matthew's voice was choked.

Many emotions played across his uncle's face as he looked at Matthew. "I am a professional soldier and I flirt constantly with the grim reaper. He is my faithful companion every time I advance into battle. His features are very familiar to me. He certainly doesn't frighten me!" His uncle took a deep breath and looked along the wall.

"Canada survives?" he asked, looking back at Matthew. "Of course it does, as you have Canada on you shoulders. Tell me about her."

Matthew sat up straight. "Canada becomes a vibrant country stretching from Halifax to the Pacific coast. I come from Vancouver, a city located on the Pacific coast." His voice was shaky. He tried hard to control it. "Canadian values, our parliamentary style of government, things that make us different from the United States are all confirmed, and reinforced by this war. We owe much of it to you, sir! Your inspired leadership instils a sense of loyalty in Canadians that survives to my time. You are knighted for your service."

His uncle extended a hand which Matthew took. His uncle's hand was warm while his was cool. Warmth smouldered in Matthew's gut, building to an intense energy which quickly pulsed up through his chest into his shoulder, then down his arm to his hand which was now feeling hot. The energy leapt the contact of hands. His uncle stiffened, his eyes glazed over, the pupils turning up, and his cheek muscles twitched. His mouth formed a hard, thin line. It was over in seconds, the energy subsided, withdrawing up Matthew's arm. Matthew's hand now felt cool. His uncle wouldn't let go.

He looked at Matthew with wide eyes, looked at his hand, and then at Matthew. At first his face was a mask of confusion which then softened to take on a friendly quality that was almost a smile. When he spoke his voice had a soft natural quality, a voice reserved for family. The voice of the general was absent.

"I give my thanks to you, for when you took my hand, my imagination ran wild. Through your eyes, your future, and Canada's future … showed … in front of my eyes! I have seen what is to come, and yes … I have seen my death! I have also seen your war and beyond it to even more trying times … for you … for Canadians … and for Canada! I do not speak to you as a general. I speak to you as your Uncle Isaac. A warning has come to me … through you … to give to you! Stand on guard for Canada, I beg of you, for enemies exist within, not just beyond her borders. These enemies call themselves leaders. They have power, patronage, and privilege. To keep from losing it, they will do anything, to the suppression of you and your neighbours … even to the break up of Canada if it suits their gain. Guard your freedoms which I saw are hard won by men like your father, my nephew, for when you lose just one freedom, without protest, you will lose them all. You have a special gift, Matthew, for inside you dwells a force, a powerful force that is evil, but evil can be turned so good comes from it. Make sure only good comes from it. You are a soldier, Matthew, a soldier that knows his duty, and when you have completed said duty you will die a happy man, as I will today. Yes, Canada becomes a great nation. Guard her, Matthew, I beg of you. Say you will and I will die with contentment in my heart."

Matthew got to his knees, losing control of his emotions, feeling his eyes tear. "I will, Uncle Isaac!" His voice was shaking as he fought to keep from breaking down.

His uncle let go of his hand and got to his feet. His soldiers did likewise. He smiled down at Matthew.

"By the way, may I inquire as to your lineage? From which of my brothers do you descend?"

"William!"

His uncle threw his head back and laughed. "Most disappointed he will be by my death for he will not be receiving any more of my funds."

With that his uncle took the bridle of his horse, went to the end of the wall, and with a yell led a frontal assault on the Americans holding the heights.

Matthew stood and looked over the wall where he saw his uncle leading his men as he charged up the hill, his sword in his hand, and leading his horse by the bridal. He brought his rifle up and laid it on top of the wall while watching the trees and bushes for movement. His mind was calm. His hands remained cool.

The Americans threw back the first charge led by his uncle. His soldiers turned and ran. His uncle shouted after them, letting his horse go free. Some of the troops stopped running and reformed into rank. Seeing this, his uncle turned to the attack, urging his men to follow.

His great great uncle was centre stage. For a brief moment a fracture in the overcast allowed a single beam of light to penetrate the battlefield. It fell directly on the general. His scarlet coat glowed, his gold epaulettes sparkled, and his sword reflected shards of light that penetrated surrounding shadow. A spotlight from heaven was focused on one of the most talented members of the cast in the drama called Canada. God, the director, was calling for the death scene. The curtain was about to fall on act one, scene one.

Matthew spotted a movement in some bushes off to the right. An American militiaman stepped from the bushes and levelled his musket at his uncle's chest. Matthew's demon was quick; its life force present in all its evil for the rational Matthew had consciously stepped aside. His vision narrowed as his breath heated and his chest heaved, the bead of his rifles fore sight glowed. He sighted and pulled the trigger, a shell being chambered since he sighted Hartenstein. The militiaman spun around with the force of the bullet, dropping his musket and falling backward to the ground.

His uncle continued his charge, the sound of muskets like hail on a tin roof. One shot sounded different. His uncle was picked off his feet and thrown backward. He hit the gravel and slid to a stop. His empty eyes stared at the sky. A trickle of blood ran from the corner of his mouth. A patch of dark reddish purple spread on the chest of his tunic. His uncle had been shot through the lungs.

The shot! It was significantly different from a musket. It had the sharp, ring-ing "crack" of a modern high velocity firearm. More like the report of a .303 cali-bre rifle. But who would have a rifle? Surely, his uncle wasn't shot by one of his men. It was impossible but it had to be. They were the only ones with .303 rifles.

A figure briefly showed on the skyline as it scrambled from behind a row of short scrub. The man paused briefly to look down at Matthew's uncle before dis-appearing over the lip of the embankment. The man wore the peaked cap and tunic of a naval officer. In the split second he was visible, Matthew picked out the lieutenant stripes on his sleeve. He recognized the familiar wood covered barrel of a .303 gripped in the man's hand.

Matthew allowed himself to slide down the wall until he was seated on the ground as realization set in. Major-General Sir Isaac Brock, hero of the War of 1812, had just been shot by a Nazi. He was shot by Hartenstein using the .303 rifle that von Friedeburg had stolen.

As his demon withdrew, its blood lust momentarily sated, Matthew's rational side pondered the conflict at the intersection where Hartenstein had pranced in the fog. Perhaps if the demon had overpowered judicious thinking his famous uncle need not have died. Perhaps there is some good to be done by irresponsible action.

CHAPTER 22

▼

Matthew took hold of his rifle and stood up. He was violently reminded to keep his head down as a musket ball chipped a piece of stone from the top of the wall a yard in front of him. He was dead tired, having been on his feet without sleep for over thirty hours. He covered a lot of territory during that time. He spotted a British tar named Newlove, who came running when Matthew called him, crouching to avoid being shot.

"We've bin looking for yuh, sir! The killick is gettin' worried."

"Where are the men, Newlove?"

"Well, we ain't no more where yuh left us, sir. It was getting right hot where we were so we moved."

"Lead me to them, Newlove. We've got to get a move on! Hartenstein is in Queenston. I just saw him, there ... on the ridge."

Newlove peered over the wall at the top of the escarpment.

"Come on, Newlove! We'd better get after him!"

"They're this way, sir."

Using the wall for cover, Newlove started moving west. Matthew followed.

The battle was quiet at the moment, only a small battery of cannon down river kept firing. The Americans were in control of the heights and most of the village. Only a few pockets of British regulars remained. Matthew led his men west between battle-scarred, abandoned dwellings, through orchards laden with ripened fruit, and gardens freshly harvested. They were soon out of the village.

Five hundred yards from the village they crossed a small stream. It was another eight hundred yards through open meadow to a road that ran north to south. They turned south and followed the road to the top of the first escarpment. Fifteen hundred yards to the east, the Americans were trying to drill out the ramrod that was broken off in the touch hole of the eighteen pound cannon. They crossed a road that ran along the ridge and scaled the second escarpment. They stopped just below the top edge.

After working their way to the edge on their knees and elbows, Matthew and the killick gunner surveyed the flat area of the heights. The killick handed a pair of binoculars to Matthew.

Matthew scanned the field. Directly east the Americans were milling about, seemingly with no direction. He estimated them to number about a thousand. He swung his binoculars to the south and stopped. He focused on a platoon of men.

"There's the bastard!" It was Hartenstein. He seemed to be having a heated discussion with another German naval officer. They were arguing in front of a platoon of men that were standing three ranks deep in advance formation with muskets at the shoulder.

Matthew pointed to a large grove of trees that was about two hundred yards away across flat open ground.

"We'll cross one at a time and reform in those trees." He patted the killick's shoulder. "You first, I'll direct the others to follow."

The killick gripped his rifle and prepared to make the dash.

"Hold up!"

The sound that came from the grove of trees sent shivers down Matthew's back and raised the short hairs on his neck. It was a howl that could not be generated within the throats of men. Suddenly, from out of the grove came a mass of screaming, whooping, swearing, and half-naked, running men. Painted and feathered, they waved muskets, hatchets, knives, and clubs as they ran.

The Americans on the escarpment above the river shrank back at the sight and sound of the attacking Mohawks. The consequences of tackling them and losing were well known by the Americans. Their officers tried to form them up to meet the Indians; they were only partly successful. A number of Americans retreated down the bank to the river.

"Okay killick, get going. We'll be right behind you."

The killick took off at a crouched run.

"Okay Parsons, you're next. Go!"

As the men left at thirty-second intervals, Matthew focused his binoculars on Hartenstein and his formation. They were directly in the path of the charging Mohawks. One of Hartenstein's militia broke ranks and started running. Hartenstein gestured. A large man stepped from the ranks and levelled his musket on the retreating back. A cloud of smoke blossomed from the musket. The running man threw his arms into the air and fell flat on his face, sliding to a stop and laying still. The large man stepped back into the ranks.

Hartenstein turned to face the advancing Mohawks. He handed his rifle, Booth's stolen rifle, to the other officer, and marched ten paces in the direction of the charging Mohawks. He stood ramrod stiff, hands on his hips, fists clenched. Suddenly, he held out his right hand in the time-honoured symbol for "stop."

Curiously, the Mohawks stopped their charge. They stopped waving their hatchets and muskets. Their arms dropped to their sides. They stood silently looking at the obviously irresponsible Hartenstein.

Hartenstein turned his back on the Mohawks, a gesture of contempt in any man's language. He shouted an order that Matthew could not hear. His men turned to the right in column of three. He gestured, again shouting an order. His men began goose-stepping. Hartenstein fell in at the head of the column and picked up the step.

The Mohawks moved aside allowing Hartenstein to march through their ranks and along the road that led south to the falls. The Mohawks stood and watched him pass. They never lifted a hand against Hartenstein. After his squad passed through the Mohawks closed ranks, raised their hatchets and clubs, and with loud war cries continued their attack on the Americans who had now formed into line to await them.

Matthew lowered his binoculars. Hartenstein must lead a charmed life. He had a power over the human mind and he exercised it to the utmost. He was either very brave and that made him foolish; or he was highly intelligent and could read the mood of men, friend or opponent, which would make him very dangerous. If Matthew was in that situation, he would have considered rapid retreat a sensible choice. Hartenstein must have decided that he didn't have a chance running so he took the only option he had. He held his cards close to his chest, bluffed, and won both the ante and the jackpot.

"Jesus! They're waiting for me." Matthew climbed over the edge and ran the two hundred yards. Worried faces broke into smiles when he stumbled, out of breath, into the grove.

Panting, he looked east where the Mohawks had made contact with the American line. He shivered at the thought of an axe splitting his head open or his scalp being ripped from his skull while he was still breathing. It would be a quicker death, he supposed, than drowning or slowly freezing in the North Atlantic. Every war had its own particular hell.

Now was the time for action but he had no idea what to do now that Hartenstein had left the field, disappearing down the same road Matthew had taken the previous day. Over the past two weeks he and his men had endured the hardships of primitive travel that modern men only pursued as sport. They had one mission, to bring Hartenstein back to Boston or leave him buried under good Canadian sod. He looked at the expectant faces of his men. They were a rag-tag group, but by God, he could rely on them. They griped and complained but cooperation and teamwork brought them to Niagara. He had to think—what was his next move?

He sat and leaned his back against a tree. Fatigue swept his body in a wave; his eyelids grew heavy. He had to keep awake. He turned to Newlove who was leaning against the tree to his left.

"What did you do on civy street, Newlove?"

"Where's civy street, sir?" Newlove spoke through a near toothless mouth, his words slurred.

He smiled at the man. "Civy street is ... well ... what were you before you joined the navy? How were you employed?"

"I was an acrobat, sir," said Newlove, showing some excitement. "I walked the high cable plying folk at fairs 'n markets. I never did accept the Kings shilling. I was pressed, had no time fer fare-thee-wells."

Matthew looked away for a kernel of an idea was forming in his mind and he needed time for it to grow. He stood up and leaned against the tree, turning his back on his men. Yes, it may work. It had to work!

"Killick, I require two men to return to Fort George for equipment. They have to hurry, because we don't have much time. Maybe they can shanghai some horses. Now ... listen up ..."

CHAPTER 23

"Hard to believe, isn't it, Bell?" Matthew was standing beside a tall pine, looking east across Niagara Falls where the full moon hung over the forests of New York State, briefly showing itself through a gap in the overcast.

"What is, Yeoman?"

"It's almost a month, you know, since we visited Boston in the middle of the night."

"Oh yeah ... but it seems like yesterday."

Matthew's gaze wandered from the spectacular Horseshoe Falls on the Canadian side to the small island that divided the falls at the Canada-United States border and on to the less spectacular American falls. Reflected ribbons of moonlight played in the black whirlpools and silver eddies above the falls. Some of them were caught and thrown over the crest to dance with the mist that rose from the basin that the falls alone created. The hand of man had not yet transformed this terrestrial splendour into a profitable silhouette where newlyweds and tourists are milked of hard earned cash. No hotels with their swimming pools and nightclubs. No telescopes mounted on cement platforms, railed off to prevent exuberant tourists from falling to their deaths. No starry eyed honeymooners sitting on park benches looking at the full moon, which, thankfully, was still out of man's reach.

Matthew's thoughts came back to his immediate problem. They worked quietly, the sound of the falls, and the ranting of Hartenstein in the meadow opposite, covered any noise they made. Matthew's assumption proved correct. Hartenstein was making the mistake of using the meadow at the intersection where he had seen him in the previous evening.

"Time?"

"Just on oh two thirty, Yeoman."

"Okay." Matthew looked up the tall pine. "Tell the other guys to stand by the line."

"Aye-aye, Yeoman." Bell moved off to where a group of seamen sat in quiet conversation. Knowing the meaning of his approach, they quickly moved to tail the one and a half inch line that led from the base of the tree and through a pair of double blocks rigged to give a four-to-one purchase.

The intersection was tee shaped, the road running to the west branching off the north-south main road. The meadow was in the southwest corner of the intersection. Matthew's pine was a hundred yards south of the intersection on the east side of the road. The line passed through a block at the base of the pine, then fed through a second block seventy-five feet up the pine. The line stretched through overhanging branches, but outside the trunks of trees, northward to a tall pine east of, but next to, the intersection. Here the line was nipped to the trunk about fifty feet up. A seaman sat on a branch with a bayonet to cut the lashings. From that tree, the line crossed the north-south road to a pine that was set up similar to Matthew's, a hundred yards west along the branch road. The *Shannon's* midshipman was in charge of that tree where a number of men stood by to tail the line. The killick gunner was posted under the tree at the intersection, holding a flashlight, and keeping an eye on his watch.

The activities in the meadow finally settled down. The bonfire was almost burned out, a few flames licked upward from the glowing embers giving charred logs a final warm embrace. Hartenstein and his legion ringed the warm embers, sleeping on ground sheets, and covered by a single blanket. Matthew could see two men sitting and looking into the fire, probably engaged in quiet conversation. They must be the sentries but they weren't keeping a good lookout.

A single beam from a flashlight lit the top of a tree at the intersection. It was only a flash but it would be visible from both directions.

"There's the signal! Come on lads; put your backs into it. Stamp and go! Stamp and go! Haul that line, lads!"

The seaman up the tree at the intersection cut the lashings that held the line. With the tension released, the seaman began running, then slowing as the weight of the line factored in.

Matthew held his breath as the line dropped to the ground at the edge of the meadow. The slack was being dragged toward the sleeping Germans. He willed his men to pull faster. The slack moved closer to the Germans, the sound of it dragging through the bushes and tall grass seemed deafening. A one and a half inch line was heavy. He hoped he hadn't miscalculated, because he had no back up. His total manpower was employed with this manoeuvre. The line continued across the meadow, skipping and thrashing, snapping small bushes. He slowly let his breath out. The loop of slack was getting smaller as the line shortened. If anyone tripped, it would be disastrous.

The line caught a bush and flipped into the air and over the outermost sleeping bodies. It continued into the air, passing a foot above the seated Germans. One looked behind him, suddenly conscious of the noise. The other raised a hand as if to swat a non-existing fly, but thankfully didn't look up.

The sailors stopped hauling, temporarily nipping the line to a sturdy tree, while the slack was fed through a series of snatch blocks to give it an eight-to-one purchase. The line climbed vertically from that point, its slack decreasing until the line was near taut at a level of seventy-five feet above the glowing embers.

"Pull, lads, pull as hard as you can." This is where the eight-to-one purchase came into play. From both ends the line was pulled until it was iron bar tight.

"Belay. Cleat off." Matthew stood back as the line was secured to a large tree. He was bathed in a sweat from the tension of the evolution. His stomach was rolling; his breathing had a slight rasping sound. He looked toward the dying fire. No one moved. This part of his plan was successful.

He looked at the sky where, thank God, the moon had disappeared behind cloud cover. It would have highlighted the line, quickly exposing the ploy. He suddenly realized that his fatigue was gone, replaced by an energy, a raw strength that was emanating, surge upon surge, from his abdomen, through his chest and groin area, and into his arms and legs. His shirt felt too small for him.

He looked up the pine where the British tar named Newlove was prepared and waiting, sitting on a branch where the line ran through the block. He was naked except for a coating of flour. Matthew's vision narrowed and focused. He was able to see Newlove clearly though it was dark and Newlove was seventy-five feet up the tree. He was able to see the mixture of excitement and fright that showed in Newlove's eyes that stared down at him. He could see the way Newlove's nostrils pinched slightly as he breathed in.

Newlove's balancing pole was fashioned from a strong sapling and rigged with two Aldis lamps, one at each end. A line attached to the trigger of each lamp ran through blocks outboard of the lamps. All he had to do was pull on the line and both lamps would illuminate him. The tree rocked back and forth with the weight of the line as he waited for the signal to move.

Matthew's muscles tensed with new found energy—a boundless power. His diaphragm sucked air into his lungs with the force of a blacksmith's bellows. His mouth was the furnace, his breath becoming hot, and his spit tasted like diesel. He reached above him and with one hand, pulled himself to the first branch. He continued up the tree, hand after hand, not bothering to seek a foothold.

"Move aside, Newlove! I won't need you." His voice had a harsh authority to it and a visibly frightened Newlove moved over a branch, leaving room at the end of the line. He took no notice of Newlove's wide, staring, and frightened eyes. No notice of Newlove shrinking away at the sight of him. He felt as if he was buoyant, climbing into an atmosphere so thick he was rendered weightless. He was immersed in sound, a cacophony of echoing voices resonating from different eras, each calling out to him, beckoning him, pleading with him to let go of his own soul, and to relinquish his body for occupation and immortality. His demon was now in residence and he could live forever. Matthew stepped onto the rope.

CHAPTER 24

▼

The sound was maniacal, demented! As wild as a coyote's howl is wild! Supernatural as the cry of a banshee is supernatural! Yet it was human, as the savage cry of an attacking Mohawk is human. It reverberated off the surrounding evergreens giving it the depth and hollowness of originating from the deep well of man's collective trepidation. It came from the night, the black curtain outside the circle of light cast by the fire. At first it came from afar, but it advanced, without pause, a continuous moan that grew to a screech as it passed overhead of the men by the fire, and receded toward the other side of the meadow. Only it returned, passing overhead at great speed to whence it came.

Then there was silence, only a moment reprieve, perhaps one minute, perhaps two, for it began again. A sound as soft as the purr of a kitten is soft, slowly building to the guttural snarl of a stalking male lion. It advanced from the northwest corner of the field with the swiftness of a passing shell before receding again to the southeast.

Then it happened. A brilliant glow in the night sky that radiated from the figure of a man lit the field and the surrounding trees. He was a menacing spectre, the harbinger of a dreadful future. He was unrestrained as a barbarian was unrestrained. His mouth was wide open, circular, emitting a cacophony of men's tongues, speaking many languages, some lost in antiquity. His breath showed as a fog. The spectre now moved as the man began walking, slowly approaching overhead of the men by the fire whose pale, terrified faces looked up at him. He stopped above them, still jabbering, with his light softly pulsing.

Below the phantom, the two men must have allowed their fear to determine their actions. One, a large man, leapt to his feet and started running, jumping over sleeping bodies, while glancing back at the apparition in the sky. His partner joined him. Sleepers awoke and were drawn into the panic, quickly becoming a stampede of scared men. Obviously, no thought was given to muskets or bayonets. No thought was given to sleeping neighbours. Men were trampled by those awake and running.

The numbers increased. Fifty, seventy-five, and then one hundred and thirty men were following the fleeing large man who was heading for the intersection. Behind and above them, the apparition disappeared, the sky returning to an empty black.

Matthew's men converged on the corner to intercept the running men. The voice of Hartenstein could be heard screaming after them. Panicky men are difficult to stop, as stampeding buffalo or runaway horses are difficult to stop. When the herding instinct takes charge, all that can be done is to wait until they fatigue. They broke through the line of Matthew's men who, on recognizing that they were the Americans, let them pass. It was the German sailors, the U-boat crew who were the ones in uniform, along with their commander, that they wished to capture.

Hartenstein and his crew were still back at the fire where the submariners were now awake and standing in two ranks, muskets in hand, under the now dark sky. Hartenstein stood in front of the glowing embers, the back lighting showing him in imposing profile, clenched fists on his hips, elbows out to the side. His mouth opened as if to shout at the men or give them an order when a voice speaking German in a commanding manner came at him from the night sky. It was a voice that Hartenstein must have recognized, for it had the tone and inflection of the person that Hartenstein, as a Nazi, would have worshiped.

He stood, not moving, with his mouth open, and his face turned to the sky. There was a muffled plop followed by a small shower of sparks. Instinct must have warned him for he began to move, but he was too late. The centre of the coals became a small balloon of ash that expanded with a force both upward and outward. Hot coals became a burning rain. Small chunks of burning wood became pinwheels. It was a brilliant display of deadly fireworks. The heat and concussion, when it came, must have been as solid as a wall, for it lifted Hartenstein from his feet, his breath a loud gasp as the wind was driven out of him. For a split second, the length of time that a photographer's flash bulb burns, his form was seen upside down in the air. The sound of maniacle laughter echoed throughout the night sky, where a thousand voices joined together in joyous celebration. It was a celebration of victory.

A light mist had formed over the meadow as the October dew evaporated under the warmth of the morning sun. The heavy overcast of the previous day was breaking up, showing patches of blue sky. Matthew tasted the freshness in the air and smiled happily. He was delighted by the success of last night's enterprise.

The stunned and frightened Americans had no idea what happened. They had straggled back in ones and twos to the only place they knew, the meadow. The crew from the U-boat were kept separate from the Americans. As the sun warmed the chilled bones of the men, Hartenstein was still incapacitated.

The German sub-lieutenant cleaned up his commander as much as possible using wet rags to soften the blood, and then using a blanket to wipe it off. Hartenstein's uniform was tattered; jagged tears revealed reddened skin where flying coals had burned him. Of the crew from the U-boat, only two were killed, a burning stave from an old barrel pierced one man through the heart. Another twelve were burned or had other injuries. The rest had splitting headaches. A number of the Americans had bruises and abrasions from being trampled.

By noon the dead were buried and Matthew and his men were moving out. The Americans and the Germans were under heavy guard. Hartenstein was carried on a stretcher fabricated from blankets secured and stretched between two poles. Darkness was falling by the time they moved into the village of Queenston. There, the Americans were turned over to Captain Dennis of the British regulars as prisoners of war.

"Will we be exchanged?" A large man, who seemed to be a leader among the Americans, asked the question.

"I'm not sure," replied Captain Dennis. "You are not part of an official United States militia. You may just have to wait out the war as prisoners in Canada." He looked at Matthew. "Hopefully, that won't be too long from now?"

They left Queenston the next morning; Matthew felt it too risky to travel at night with his German prisoners. Besides that, he was fugging exhausted. At Fort George, the prisoners were confined in the stockade. The ailing Hartenstein, along with the other wounded, were taken to hospital, such as it was, where they remained under guard.

It was time to relax, celebrate with a few ales, perhaps a keg of rum. Booth was a very happy sailor for he now had his rifle back.

Matthew broke away from his men and walked alone to a quiet location. He stood in silence and looked at Fort George and the log building where he'd first met his great great uncle. He wiped the single tear that escaped from his right eye and ran down his cheek. He mouthed his words so that only he would hear them. He felt blessed to be able to say them.

"Good-bye, Uncle Isaac." His voice broke. "It was an honour to meet you!"

CHAPTER 25

▼

November 1812 began with the weather turning bitterly cold for the time of year. The town of New York, confined to the southern two-thirds of Manhattan Island, snuggled down in a warm blanket of coal and wood smoke. Its inhabitants had already started the long standing American tradition of blaming Canadians for the cold wind that swept down the Hudson River to infiltrate the streets and alleys and invade dwellings and businesses.

During the night Matthew and his flotilla, wrapped-up as best they could to keep out the cold, passed Battery Park as they rounded the southern tip of Manhattan Island. Matthew chose not to travel to the East River using Harlem Creek. It was best to avoid detection and curious inquiries.

A bitter off-shore wind turned the harbour into a maze of white caps making it rough going, but it was better than being noticed. Hartenstein was tucked away aft in Matthew's cutter under constant guard. The German sub-lieutenant was guarded in the same manner on the killick gunner's cutter. The U-boat crew was under the guard of British tars and divided between the whaler and one freighter canoe, each on a tow from a diesel cutter.

Daylight found the flotilla passing Throgs Neck, leaving the East River and entering the wider expanse of Long Island Sound. They'd waited for slack water before passing through Hell Gate, a narrow strip of water on the East River known for its strong tidal currents and back eddies. Now the tide was with them and their speed over bottom was around eight knots. The bitter wind had slackened making the trip much more palatable. Wind or no wind, all were in high spirits as they looked forward to the warm mess deck on *Blackfoot*.

"Let's rig the wireless, Bell, and see if we can raise *Blackfoot*."

"Aye-aye, Yeoman," said Bell with obvious enthusiasm. He took the lashings off two poles which had the antenna strung between them and attached to insulators. With a screwdriver, Matthew undid the covers that were fitted over pre-drilled holes in the bow and stern of the cutter. The base of each pole was passed through a hole and into a tabernacle beneath the deck where the pole was made snug tight.

The radio set came next, the same one that they'd rigged on *Shannon*. It was unpacked from its waterproof container and plugged into its battery pack that was stored separately. Crossing his fingers, Matthew flicked the power switch to "on" and waited patiently for the set to warm up. The battery pack was still good. He connected the microphone, selected the correct frequency, and tuned the antenna.

"Well, here goes." He licked his lips, having to think for a second to remember his call sign. Oh yeah, his initials.

"*Blackfoot … Blackfoot … Blackfoot …* this is Mike Bravo … Mike Bravo … Mike Bravo … radio check, over."

All he could hear was static. He tried again but *Blackfoot* didn't acknowledge.

"What's the time, Bell?"

"Zero nine twenty-two, Yeoman."

"I guess we'll have to wait till noon when *Blackfoot* is scheduled to call us." He switched off. They were probably still out of range. In a few hours they should be in contact. However, there was another matter to attend to.

He took his binoculars and focused on the paddle wheel vessel that had been following astern since they began their passage up the East River. It seemed to be tailing them, maintaining a specific distance throughout the night, and so far, throughout the morning. He studied the vessel, feeling that he'd seen it before. Yes! It was on the Hudson when he was heading up river. The vessel was the *Clermont*, a passenger vessel that was most likely on route to a village along the coast.

Matthew lowered his binoculars, but as he turned away, something caught his eye. There were two flashes on the steam vessel. Were they reflection of sunlight off polished metal? Or was it an intentional signal—to someone—somewhere? He would have dismissed it as a reflection but something inside him stirred, a movement that he'd learned over the past month to pay attention to. It was telling him that the flashes were intentional. He re-focused his binoculars on the *Clermont*. Again, two flashes five seconds apart.

Was the signal directed to him? Did they want him to stop? He decided to slow down and see what reaction he got from the vessel. He signalled his intention to the killick gunner, and then he ordered the stoker to reduce revolutions.

Yes! The range was closing! Whoever it is must want to—wait a minute! The steam vessel had reduced speed and was taking up station at its original distance. Obviously they were following and not wanting to make contact. It could only be one person with the motivation to follow—a person who expressed an intense interest in the power plant of *Blackfoot*. That person was Robert Fulton! Well, the fellow was simply wasting his fugging time because the Old Man won't let him have what he wants. Matthew ordered the stoker to increase speed and upon seeing the increased wake, the killick gunner also increased speed.

The cutter's diesel coughed, clanked and rattled. The steam vessel puffed, snorted, hissed and thrashed. The sun silently climbed the eastern sky toward its apex. At five minutes to noon, Matthew switched on the wireless, tuned the antenna, checked all connections and confirmed the frequency setting. Was *Blackfoot* still there—still waiting for them?

"Two sailing vessels approaching from the mainland, bearing red three zero, Yeoman."

"Thanks, Bell." Matthew focused his binoculars on the sailing vessels. One was a gaff-rigged schooner of the New England style. It had a long clipper bow with two masts that swept aft at a rakish angle. The second vessel was a small gaff rigged sloop. Wait! There's something unusual about the sloop. It was on the port tack and heeled to starboard which allowed Matthew to look directly at its deck. It had no cockpit for its deck was clean from bow to stern, broken only by the mast and a small circular structure that looked like a large over-turned pail. Only three men were visible on deck.

He turned to study the *Clermont*, seeing activity on its foredeck where men were busily working around a large crate near the bow.

"Mike Bravo … Mike Bravo … Mike Bravo … this is … *Blackfoot* … *Blackfoot* … *Blackfoot*." The quiet conversation of the men in the cutter quickly turned to excitement. Broad, happy smiles lit up their faces.

"Let's have some silence!" Matthew was barely able to contain his own excitement as he waited until they'd quieted down. He picked up the mike.

"*Blackfoot* … *Blackfoot* … *Blackfoot* … this is Mike Bravo … Mike Bravo … Mike Bravo … radio check, over."

"This is *Blackfoot* … great to hear you, Matt. You are readable with some static. State your position, over."

"Our position is Long Island sound with Eatons Neck bearing … stand-by one." What the hell? A column of water rose fifteen feet to port, followed by a loud bang. Cannon fire! He stuck his head through the hatch and looked astern where a cloud of smoke hid the bow of the steam vessel.

"This is Mike Bravo! We are under attack! I say again ... we are under attack! Stand by ... over!"

"This is *Blackfoot* ... roger. I will inform the captain of your situation. *Blackfoot* standing by ... out."

"Christ!" When the smoke cleared from the bow of the *Clermont* Matthew saw that the large crate was removed and a naval cannon was exposed, aimed slightly to starboard to avoid hitting *Clermont's* bowsprit. Men were busy reloading for another shot. He stood in stunned silence, his mind unable to grasp the situation, his stomach churning. He looked toward the sailing vessels and saw that they'd let out their sheets and were bearing towards him with bones in their teeth. The schooner was rapidly pulling away from the sloop.

What the hell was Fulton trying to do? In no way would it advance his cause. One thing Matthew did know, he'd better start defending his flotilla. He wasn't about to surrender to a power hungry, money hungry, egotistic but famous Yankee. Certainly not after having tramped his way to Niagara and capturing Hartenstein without firing a shot, then to make their way back to the Hudson River. Perhaps it is because Canada and the United States are at war and Matthew and his flotilla are British and Canadian sailors loose in enemy waters.

"We will see how far we can carry this little war, Mister Fulton," said Matthew with defiance. He turned to Booth who was on the tiller. "Cast off the fugging tow!"

CHAPTER 26

▼

Matthew's cutter picked up speed without the tow.

"Hard to port ... take her up to full revolutions ... let's see what this fugging tub can do!" Matthew was clenching his jaw so hard his teeth hurt. The cutter heeled to starboard with the tightness of the turn.

"Steady." He cupped his hands to his mouth as he passed the killick gunner's cutter. "Keep an eye on my tow. I suggest you pass out ammunition." The killick waved his acknowledgment.

He focused on the naval cannon on *Clermont's* bow, keeping his eye on the lay of the barrel. The *Clermont's* gunner was waiting with lanyard in hand for them to cut across his line of fire. "When I say "now," I want a hard turn to starboard."

Matthew watched the gunner who would be figuring his deflection before firing. Any moment now! He saw the gunner tense his lanyard.

"Now!" The cutter skidded with the sharpness of the turn. At the same moment, the cannon erupted with smoke and flame. Matthew felt the wind from the passing ball.

"Head straight for the fugging cannon!" He would be there before the gun crew had time to reload. Right now the gunner would be kicking his own ass.

The men working the cannon abandoned the gun, picked up their muskets and crouched, resting their weapons on the low bulwarks. Matthew directed Bell's attention to one that remained standing.

"Let's see how your aim is, Bell."

Matthew noticed Bell's hand was shaking as he fed a shell into the chamber of his .303. He laid the rifle across the forward sliding canopy, sighted the rifle while his finger felt for the trigger. Matthew was watching him. All in the cutter, who could see him, were watching him. Bell started to shake, losing his aim. Matthew mentally urged him on, knowing that this would be Bell's first kill. He would know what it was like to take a life, the inexplicable feelings shoved to the back of his mind that must be dealt with! Now was not the time! Later! Maybe never!

Bell sighted again, took a deep breath, then lifted his cheek from the rifle stock and brushed his eyes with his shirt sleeve which came away wet. His target had spotted the rifle and was moving for cover. Bell was suddenly and roughly shoved aside, the rifle was pulled from his grip. Newlove had come from under the aft canopy and taken the rifle from him.

Newlove quickly assumed firing position, aimed the rifle and pulled the trigger, his shoulder thrown back by the recoil. His target assumed a crouching position but without his brains which were now a fine mist in the air behind him. Newlove turned to look at the sweating, shaking Ordinary Seaman Bell, his grin showing the gaps in his teeth.

Bell stared back defiantly. "I would'a fired."

"It's okay, laddy," said Newlove. "Nothing wrong with you that a tot o' rum wouldn't fix."

The men behind the *Clermont's* bulwarks fell back along the deck on their hands and knees, dragging their muskets beside them. Newlove raised the .303.

"Belay that," said Matthew, who winced, having just been punched in the stomach from the inside. "One is enough … for now."

The *Clermont* began a turn to port, presenting its starboard side to Matthew's approach. The gun crew were now sheltered behind the structure that shrouded the starboard paddle wheel. Matthew pulled onto a parallel course approximately fifty yards off. He turned to Bell.

"Cover me."

Bell looked at him with his mouth open, his eyes full of questions, then at Newlove who was holding out the rifle. His face hardened as he took the rifle and assumed a firing position, working the bolt action. Matthew climbed onto the aft canopy.

"Ahoy the *Clermont*. Robert Fulton … I wish to speak with Robert Fulton." He waited, one minute, two minutes—he was about to call again when a figure moved from under the poop. The man was wearing a tall hat, a long winter cloak, and his hands were not visible. It was Fulton. Matthew took a deep breath.

"Mister Fulton … this is Matthew Brock. What the hell are you trying to do?"

Fulton didn't answer. He looked back at where he came from, then back at Matthew. He brought his right hand from behind his cloak and waved as to a friend. He then moved back under the poop.

"Well shit!" Fulton looked worried! Frightened perhaps? What the hell does Fulton have up his sleeve? He was quickly answered.

From across the water came the sound of rifle fire followed by the heavy concussion of naval cannon. Matthew spun around at the sound. A musket ball slammed into the woodwork beneath his feet.

Bell fired just as the man who had shot at Matthew disappeared behind the paddle wheel's covering structure. Splinters flew from the edge of the structure, the passing bullet continuing on to slice through a pressurized steam pipe. The pipe ruptured with a popping sound followed by the "whoosh" of escaping steam that obscured the structure but couldn't shut out the tortured screams of men scalding to death. A hideous death, a stoker's death—their skin blistering and peeling, their exposed flesh cooked with the seconds it takes for a man to die. Inside him, his demon rejoiced, Matthew's hands and abdomen felt warm. Matthew knew what was inside him; his great great uncle had understood and warned him. He consciously willed the demon to stay, mentally caging it and locking its door.

Matthew looked at the *Clermont*; the paddle wheels were coming to a stop. The screams were gone but the hiss of escaping steam continued. Bell hid his face with his hands. He was sobbing. Bell will have to live with this for the rest of his life. He turned his attention back toward the American schooner.

The killick gunner was in trouble, his cutter sinking from a ragged hole in its side. Ordinary Seaman Parsons was on the stern, hand over hand hauling on the whaler's painter, musket balls picking at his clothes, and throwing up small splashes in the water around him. It looked as if the killick was going to abandon the cutter by transferring into the whaler. The American schooner ignored the killick, sweeping past the sinking cutter towards the whaler where *Shannon's* midshipman was directing his men to fire on the vessel. A single cannon fired, its blast of smoke running along the side of the speeding schooner. The midshipman was lifted into the air, his body an unrecognizable pulp when it fell into the water. In the whaler, British tars were lacerated; bits of body, brain matter and shreds of smoking clothes formed a grisly mist that hung in the air over the holed whaler, before falling into the water as a repulsive rain. Only five men escaped the dreadful blast of grape shot, who quickly abandoned the sinking whaler to swim through the floating stew that had been their mates. One of the survivors had never learned to swim and sank like a stone, his raised left hand the last part of him to disappear. The whaler with its morbid remnants quickly filled and sank.

The schooner rounded into the wind and hove-to near the freighter canoe that had the German crew on board, the British guards leapt into the water, letting their muskets sink to the bottom of the sound. Matthew saw a German sailor quickly untie the painter that led to the sinking whaler. A line sailed through the air from the stopped schooner, which was caught and secured to the canoe. The canoe was then pulled to the side of the waiting schooner.

So that's it! Fulton is after the German crew and *Clermont* had effectively done its job by attracting attention to it. Matthew looked to where his freighter canoe, filled with German sailors, bobbed in the fetch. The Germans had overpowered their guards, kept their muskets, and pitched the guards overboard. They waited to be picked up by the schooner.

Matthew looked for the sloop. It was nowhere to be seen, having literally disappeared from the surface of Long Island Sound. He tasted bile in his mouth. He never thought himself much of a warrior, or a violent person—but he was consumed with hate, which fed the demon, who was rattling the bars of its cage. Over half his men had been slaughtered—and all for Fulton's profit motive. Damn it! It was time for aggressive action! The survivors must be ignored until the battle was won. His abdomen was kicked hard from the inside and he doubled over. His demon was angry from being kept locked away. Now, with his anger, Matthew mentally unlocked its cage, and it burst forth with full fury, kicking open the heavy, barred door. Power surged to Matthew's arms and legs, his vision narrowed and became keenly focused, his breath was hot and his mouth tasted like diesel. He jumped off the canopy and alongside Bell who backed away in fear, for this was a different yeoman.

"Stand by to board!" His voice consisted of many voices, issuing from many throats, echoing through the caverns of time. He bent down to look under the aft canopy where the tars were busy with their weapons. At the rear, still under guard, was the leering visage of Hartenstein, a look of triumph in his eyes. Matthew met his gaze, reached out and drew the Nazi in to let him see the hate that existed within this seemingly docile Canadian. Hartenstein stiffened, his face showed anxiety; he struggled as he tried to break the contact. Matthew let him go and Hartenstein fell back hard, hitting his head on the aft end of the canopy. He collapsed where he sat. He'd pissed himself.

"Take us alongside, Booth, and don't look at me! Watch where you're going! Keep an eye open for movement, Bell. If you see any, shoot, don't ask fugging questions, just shoot! The time to be nice ... is over!"

CHAPTER 27

▼

Matthew's cutter covered the three hundred feet to the *Clermont* in less than a minute. An American, whose obvious intention was to die a heroic death, ran from under the poop, crouched and levelled his musket at the approaching cutter. He died where he crouched, simultaneously hit by four bullets.

Matthew, a Browning 9mm pistol in hand, leapt to the bulwarks of the *Clermont* before the cutter was within four feet. The rest followed on the heels of Matthew, only the stoker and the man guarding Hartenstein remained on board.

The large double wheel wasn't manned. An ornately decorated bulkhead crossed from port to starboard under the forward edge of the poop, separating the cabins from the quarterdeck. Double doors were located on the ships centre line. Matthew focused on those doors.

"Cripps, take two men and clear the forward deck. Booth, take a man and clear the poop. The rest of you … follow me!"

He ran for the doors, his energy fortifying his left shoulder, his muscles a hardened battering ram, his breath now volcanic—audible over the noise of escaping steam. The heavily built doors splintered when he put his shoulder into them and he threw himself into the passage in a tucked roll. A musket ball passed over him at chest height catching one of his followers in the upper arm, shattering the bone. Matthew came up in a semi-kneeling position, his pistol level, and pumped three bullets into the man who fired the musket. The man died, surprise masking his features, his wide-open eyes staring at Matthew. The beast that is Matthew laughed the hideous cackles of old hags gathered at the base of a guillotine, waiting for the blade to drop, their final farewell to the victim. Laughs that reverberated from just one horror of man's history emanating from Matthew's mouth, for the beast was there.

The passage was lined with doors that entered port and starboard cabins, the captain's cabin being aft. Matthew's men began kicking open cabin doors. He walked slowly and deliberately toward the captain's cabin, eyes narrowly focused on the doorknob, his hearing keen. He could hear every breath, every nose that sniffed, every blink of an eye, and every scratch of fingers made by the occupants of the cabin. Musket shots rang loud in the confined space of the side cabins as the tars gave no quarter; their anger was so deep. Matthew's anger, his beast's anger, radiated a sphere of influence affecting those close to Matthew, those who fought alongside Matthew. An American, who had raised his hands in surrender, was thrown against a side cabin bulkhead by the force of the bullet that passed through his lung. He collapsed, sliding down the wall, his eyes pleading. He tried to speak but only a red froth escaped his lips. The man died not understanding the hatred that was felt toward him.

Matthew's acute hearing detected five men in the captain's cabin. There were two directly behind the door, one off to the starboard side, and two near the centre at the back of the cabin. One had a cough that was muffled. He flattened himself against the passage bulkhead a split second before two musket balls ripped through the door. Quickly and with demon force, he kicked the door with his right foot, sending it off its hinges and across the cabin. It took the two men who had fired the shots and flattened them against the sharp edge of the captain's desk, snapping their spines before tearing them in half, their intestines spilling across the desk and onto the rich carpet. The door cartwheeled before smashing through the cabin's stern windows.

Matthew did a tuck and roll into the cabin. A musket fired on his right, the ball passing over him. He rolled to his feet and fired his pistol twice, hitting the man first in the left shoulder, the second shot making a neat hole in the man's forehead. The ejected shell casings rolled across the floor and up against Fulton's left shoe. The man was dead; the back of his head left a bloody pattern on the gaudy wallpaper that lined the cabin.

"Hold it!" Matthew grabbed a musket from a tar, stopping him from killing Fulton. Fulton was tied to a chair and guarded by a man who was holding a pistol to Fulton's head. Ignoring his men who quickly gathered in the cabin, Matthew stared at the man, the demon's stare that rendered the man incapable of moving. He walked behind the man, raised his pistol and placed the barrel against the nap of the man's neck, and he laughed. It was the insane laugh of Caligula as he tore open his pregnant wife's abdomen, for the beast was there. It was mixed with the triumphant laugh of Napoleon when he marched from exile into France, for the beast was there, in both places, at both times! Fulton, who was visibly shaking, was hit with a fit of coughing when he caught the stench of Matthew's breath. The front of his white shirt was speckled with blood. The pistol that was being held to his head, dropped to the deck.

Late afternoon found Matthew on the bridge of *Blackfoot*, which had the disabled *Clermont* rafted to its starboard side. He was giving the Old Man a verbal report of the action when a voice pipe interrupted him.

"ASDIC … Bridge."

The Jimmy, who had been standing, puffing his pipe and listening to Matthew's report with interest, answered. "Bridge … ASDIC." He bent to put his ear close to the funnel shaped voice pipe. His countenance changed from boredom to astonishment. "You're … listen, if this is some kind of a joke … okay! Put it on the bridge repeater!"

The Jimmy straightened and looked at the Old Man. "Submarine, sir!"

The bridge repeater came to life, it's "ping" followed almost instantly by an echo

The Old Man bent to the voice pipe. "Bridge … ASDIC … this is the captain." He listened, then straightened and crossed the bridge to the port side and shaded his eyes. The reflection of the late afternoon sun and associate glare off the water made any surface disturbance invisible. He walked back to the voice tube. "Bridge … ASDIC. What is the range and bearing?" He listened a minute, then looked at Matthew.

"Apparently the contact is quite small but partly metallic. Would you know anything, Yeoman?"

Of course, it was the sloop, the vessel that went missing before the start of action.

"It may be one of Fulton's diving boats, sir. The sloop I reported seeing earlier, which disappeared, may have submerged. That must be it!"

The Old Man stared at him before looking off to port. "Well, then perhaps it's time to teach that pest a lesson … a lesson from the future. He wants to know about the future, doesn't he?" He looked back at Matthew. "Return to the *Clermont* and order all on board to abandon the vessel and come on board *Blackfoot*, including this Hartenstein fellow. Have two men man the cutter; we'll bring it aboard later. Just get it away from the *Clermont*."

"Aye-aye, sir!" Matthew turned, left the bridge and descended to the weather deck where he scrambled down a rope ladder to the *Clermont's* deck.

"Bell … Booth … stand by to cast off, and then take the cutter. You'll be picked up later. Newlove, bring Hartenstein from the cutter and put him on board *Blackfoot* … and Newlove, guard him carefully. The rest of you, come aboard. Mister Fulton … you come with me!"

Fulton looked up at *Blackfoot's* bridge and smiled.

"I wouldn't get my hopes up, if I was you, Mister Fulton."

Hartenstein was taken below to the brig where the German sub-lieutenant already resided. The killick gunner, Cripps, Parsons, and a number of tars, were picked up earlier by *Blackfoot*. They had been floating with no means of propulsion in the freighter canoe abandoned by the U-boat crew.

"Cast off." The Old Man watched as Bell and Booth cast off the lines. Then they ran to the cutter. "Stand by to depth charge!"

"Jesus! No … please … I beg you!" Fulton, who Matthew had escorted to the bridge, put his hands together in a prayer position. "The men … think of the men!"

The Old Man looked at Fulton, his face showing his disgust with the man. He went to the voice pipes. "Bridge … engine room." He listened. "Chief, let's have ten turns of the screw and no more."

From the thrust of the screw, the two vessels began to drift apart. Matthew could see that the Old Man didn't want to alert the men in the diving boat with propeller noise. It took at least fifteen minutes before he saw a disturbance on the surface of the water to port of the *Clermont*. The two ships were now fifty yards apart. He was able to make out something floating just under the surface, something that was leaving a wake as if under its own power, heading straight for the paddle wheeler.

Matthew approached the Old Man. "Sir, there's something near the surface to port of the *Clermont*. It is moving toward her."

The Old Man moved to the port side and looked at the water.

Matthew pointed. "Over there, sir, just below the surface."

The Old Man focused his binoculars on the disturbance before looking back at Matthew. "Bring Fulton here."

"Aye-aye, sir." Matthew turned but Fulton was already near but hanging back, his mouth was working. Matthew could see sweat on his forehead. He signalled Fulton to come.

"Fulton's here, sir."

The Old Man faced Fulton and pointed at the disturbance. "Explain yourself!"

Fulton coughed into his handkerchief, and then mopped his forehead before answering. "It isn't my doing!" He saw the anger in the Old Man's eyes, and then added, "It's a torpedo!"

"Just how does it work?"

"It is pulled by the diving boat with a line. The line feeds through an eye on a spike. The crew inside can drive the spike into the bottom of a ship. They then pull the torpedo—"

"Okay, I get the picture."

Matthew watched Fulton's torpedo as it moved tediously slow, advancing across the surface in a series of jerks. The men in the diving boat must be sweating buckets, no fresh air, and no ventilation. Primitive, but he knew that this was how underwater warfare got its start.

The Old Man continued. "But … *Blackfoot* is made of steel. How would you drive the spike into her bottom?"

"It is not their intention to drive the spike into the bottom of *Blackfoot*. Through their scope they must have seen *Clermont* rafted to the side of *Blackfoot*. It must be their intention to sink *Blackfoot*." Fulton turned, his attention grabbed by the muffled thumping coming from the bilges of the *Clermont*. "Oh God … no!" Again Fulton mopped his brow.

Matthew saw that the torpedo was stopped. It wallowed in the slop. He felt an admiration for Fulton. His inventions were crude, but they were a beginning. The men, who had him captive, must have been prepared for all possibilities, even for the arrival of *Blackfoot*.

The thumping coming from under the *Clermont* ceased. Fulton's torpedo, which had floated sideways to its course from current and fetch, suddenly turned and pointed directly at the *Clermont*, and was again moving through the water.

Fulton was reduced to whimpering while sweating profusely, continually mopping his forehead. When the torpedo touched the side of the *Clermont*, he let out a moan.

There was a lick of flame followed by an explosion, the torpedo disintegrated. The force of the discharge drove a hole in the side of the vessel; the port side paddle wheel was blown from its axle to flail across the water like a cartoon duck, describing an arc before sinking. The ragged edges of boards caught fire from the heat, the flames soon spreading to the paint and tar, licking along the side and across the deck. The structure that housed the paddle wheel became a raging inferno.

The Old Man turned to the sobbing Fulton. "You know, Mister Fulton, I have a grudging respect for you. It was a near run thing. If the ASDIC wasn't being given its daily check, your torpedo would have hit *Blackfoot*."

At first, Fulton didn't answer the Old Man; he just stared at the *Clermont*. He then muttered, "It wasn't my idea!"

There was a disturbance on the surface a hundred yards to starboard of the burning vessel. As Matthew watched, a wooden vessel that was flat decked with a sailing hull rose to the surface. A hatch on top of the small metal conning tower opened releasing the inside atmosphere—a visible wave that distorted the background as it mixed with the fresh air. Three men tumbled onto the deck, gasping for breath, their clothes sticking to their bodies. One of them pointed and all three stood looking at the burning steam vessel.

"Slow ahead," said the Old Man. He was suddenly shoved aside by Fulton.

"You stupid oafs,"—Fulton shook a fist at the three men—"look what you've done. Look what you've done to my *Clermont!*" The men on the diving vessel heard his yells, saw *Blackfoot* for the first time and swung into action.

A mast with sail and booms which were lashed to the deck were raised using a block and tackle arrangement and fastened to a tabernacle; shrouds and stays were quickly attached to chain plates. The gaff rigged main sail was promptly raised and the vessel fell off on the port tack, running with the breeze. The foresail was hanked onto the head stay and raised, luffing until it was controlled by the starboard sheet. The undersea boat had become the gaff rigged sailing sloop that Matthew had seen earlier.

Guns looked at the Old Man with expectation.

"Let them go, Guns. They won't be bothering us again." The Old Man watched the diving vessel as it tacked. "At least not for a hundred years." The Old Man sat in his chair.

A loud hissing sound came from the burning steam vessel. As Matthew watched, the boiler exploded. Splinters of wood rose into the air. The burning pieces left a spiral trail of smoke behind them as they curved through the air to splash with an extinguishing hiss. The steam vessel was now in two halves. In unison, the bow and stern halves seemed to dip in a final gesture of farewell, before settling beneath the surface. Only floating debris, wood, and dead bodies were left to be disturbed by the bubbles that escaped the sinking hull.

"You know, Mister Brock, with my *Clermont* the profitability of steam powered transport was proven, for through five seasons she provided service on the Hudson." Fulton put his hand over his heart, his face neutral, showing an acceptance of what had happened. "If there be a prayer, Mister Brock, for the soul of a sinking ship, I should say it now."

"Well, Mister Fulton ... the *Clermont* will be remembered in history. And I ask you,"—he put a hand on Fulton's shoulder—"what better epitaph could there be?"

CHAPTER 28

▼

The English Captain turned from *Shannon's* stern windows where he was picking dead leaves from his plants. "Ah, Mister Brock ... I am happy to see you. As you see, I am an amateur botanist, and I find it most therapeutic." He indicated a chair facing his desk. "You have a report needing my attention?"

"Yes, sir, I do." Matthew reached into his tunic and withdrew a brown envelope and passed it across the desk. Before opening the envelope, the English Captain looked toward a door off to the starboard side of his cabin, his finger giving the "come" signal. Matthew looked at the door but couldn't see any indication of anyone being there.

The door burst open and a tar padded across the canvas-covered deck in his bare feet. On a tray he carried two crystal glasses and a carafe of claret which he placed on the desk, and then he turned and left the cabin the way he came. The English Captain filled both glasses and passed one to Matthew which he gratefully accepted.

Matthew sipped his claret as he watched the emotions play on the English Captain's face as he read the report, which was long, Matthew having written most of it, the Old Man adding his bit about the activity with the *Clermont*.

The English Captain suddenly looked at Matthew. "Oh, I have a letter for you to read, not that there is any action required of you, 'tis your opinion that I petition." He opened his top drawer and withdrew folded papers. "I usually never solicit opinions of warrant officers,"—he handed the papers to Matthew—"but from you I find a sense of purpose."

"Thank you, sir." Matthew never expected a compliment from this man and he found he was actually flattered. He took the folded papers and read the address written upon the outer fold. It was addressed to the Commander of the United States Frigate *Chesapeake*. He unfolded the papers and saw that it was a letter of two pages. He read the contents. Shit! The English Captain was challenging the American Captain.

Matthew looked at the English Captain who was still reading. He was beginning to wonder about the man's sanity for challenging the American Captain to a duel at sea. The letter actually described *Shannon's* armament and outlined areas on the ocean where they could meet.

Matthew took a sip of claret to clear his throat. This letter was a breach of security which goes against all Matthew stood for, all he'd practiced since he was an OD signalman. He needed security clearance to read such a paper, for God's sake!

Below the English Captain's signature was a postscript where he guaranteed that the steam powered warship of Canada would not interfere.

Matthew placed the letter on the desk. The English Captain finished reading the report, put it on the desk next to the letter, stood up and walked to a stern window, which framed the sun setting over Boston harbour. The lighthouse on the small island south of the Brewster chain could be seen sending its warning beam into the encroaching dusk.

"Fulton!" The English Captain spat the name. "You brought him aboard with you?"

"Yes I did, sir. He is under guard on the quarterdeck. The two Nazi officers are locked up on *Blackfoot*. Commander Forron didn't want Fulton on his ship."

"Well, what notion, may I ask, makes your captain think I desire him on mine?"

Matthew didn't answer.

"I may have use for him." The English Captain looked at the letter he'd written to the American Captain. "As to his motive, were you able to find a reason?"

"It turns out that Fulton was a captive. Others with the similar intention of capitalizing on future secrets had forced him to let them use the *Clermont* and his diving boat. Apparently, they were acquaintances of him, who, on hearing his stories of the undersea boat and *Blackfoot*, decided to profit for themselves. It was their intention to liberate the Nazi crew, which they did, but they didn't intend to get themselves killed or captured. With the Nazis, they meant to liberate the undersea boat from Boston Harbour and take it to sea. Their plan was to sink *Shannon*, then analyze the undersea boat's systems for their future use and profit."

"And what were their plans for your vessel?"

"Since Commander Forron flatly refused to educate Fulton in the propulsion system on *Blackfoot* … and being told of her incredible fire-power … they'd written her off. Although they didn't expect her to show up … they seemed prepared, however, for that possibility.

"God's truth … a mite complicated … but—" The English Captain shrugged.

"There was no risk for them, sir, or at least that's what they thought. If you don't mind my saying so, I think Fulton paid dearly for their antics. He'll probably keep his mouth shut in the future." Matthew laughed. "I suppose he could write his loses off as a business expense."

"I don't understand."

"You know, sir … income tax?"

The English Captain smiled. "No, I don't know. It must be a quirk of your time." He refilled his and Matthew's glass.

"What do you intend to do with him, sir?"

"There's a duty I have for him to perform. If he refuses,"—the English Captain stood behind his desk—"I will hang him!"

"But … but … he's innocent of any intent!"

"Innocent … no, he is not." The English Captain sat down and laid his hands flat on the desk. "He is a civilian of the worst kind. He's a spy! A decade ago he tried to profit by aiding our enemy. Aye … hang him and be damned!"

Matthew sat in stunned silence.

"I must congratulate you, for you have showed imagination and resolve."

Matthew brightened. "Thank you, sir, but a lot is owed to Newlove of your ship's company. He was a lot of help to me."

"Yes, and I will reward him, to be sure. I will inform the officer of his watch of my decision … when I've decided." The English Captain picked up his letter. "Do you have any comments?"

"Well …" He decided against saying what he actually thought. "It's not something I would do, but"—he shrugged—"who am I to change history?"

Matthew had one problem for which he had received a dressing down by the Old Man. When they did a count of the rifles, one was missing. How or where it had gone missing, he had absolutely no idea. It probably sank in the channel. Anyway, the Old Man did congratulate him on his capture of Hartenstien and his sub-lieutenant. He had successfully completed one part of his responsibily. Now, the question is what to do about the U-boat. Matthew suggested that it be towed out to sea and blown up. The question is, though, who would tow it—certainly not *Blackfoot*. Her existance is unknown to the good citizens of Boston.

"These are great beans." Ordinary seaman Bell polished off his bowl, wiping it with a crust of homemade bread that was soft and fresh from the oven. "The nickname for Boston probably originated right here in the Sign of the Lamb Tavern." He handed his bowl to the proprietor and asked for more.

"Damn it, Bell. Remember that we are back on board the *Shannon*. Your hammock is only a few inches from your neighbours. Fart and you will be sitting on the bowsprit." Matthew looked at the proprietor who was wiping tears from his eyes while trying to smile at Matthew's joke. The proprietor and Ulrich von Friedeburg were close friends and he was deeply saddened by Matthew's news of his friend's death. The proprietor's ample wife could be heard blubbering in the kitchen. However, the proprietor was relieved to hear about the capture of Hartenstien, so Matthew and Bell could eat all they wanted, and it was on the house.

Matthew and Bell were at the Sign of the Lamb tavern to wait for a reply by the American Captain to the English Captain's letter. Fulton's duty was to deliver the letter to the *Cheaspeake's* captain.

"Don't worry about me, Yeoman. If I eat enough of these beans, I won't have to chew through that rock hard beef they serve."

Matthew concentrated on his venison steak. The lad had a point there.

"As to my challenge, his reply is in the affirmative,"—the English Captain looked at Matthew—"with conditions, of course. I am to surrender the German prisoners to him to be tried by American justice for murder." The English Captain stomped his foot with glee.

"With respect, sir, I don't believe Commander Forron will let them go. They are from our time and our war. They are our prisoners of war and they are protected by convention. They have nothing to do with the *Chesapeake's* Captain."

"They may be from your time, but they murdered innocent people in my time." The English Captain paced the width of his cabin, smiling happily, perhaps at the prospect of the forthcoming battle. Matthew sat in silence.

"*Shannon* and the *Chesapeake* must meet, so I will surrender them to him. I will write orders instructing your captain to have them transferred to this vessel by eight bells of the morning watch."

What would the Old Man do? He was ordered to give up his prisoners for the selfish motives of a superior officer. If the Old Man wished, he could wash his hands of the English Captain and just steam away after recalling Matthew and his crew. The English Captain couldn't do anything about it. Matthew bet that he wouldn't do it though. The old man's pusser sense of duty would prevent him.

Sure enough, the next morning, under guard, Hartenstein and the sub-lieu-tenant were delivered to the *Shannon*. The Old Man rationalized his decision by saying that Hartenstien and the sub-lieutenant had committed conspiracy against the United States of America, a nation that wasn't at war with Germany, there-fore, they should be judged by Americans. They were going to face American mil-itary justice and the American Captain would be their judge. There would be no jury.

CHAPTER 29

▼

"Is there any statement you wish to make before I pass sentence?" The American Captain was in full dress uniform, resplendent in his dark blue tunic with stiff collar, accented with gold braid and epaulettes. The civilians in attendance were dressed in their Sunday best, including the proprietor of the Sign of the Lamb tavern who had delivered a very eloquent testimony. Matthew was there along with Bell. Both were called as witnesses. Robert Fulton was there, with his top hat in hand and his cloak thrown over his shoulder. The trial was being held in the American Captain's cabin aboard the *Chesapeake*.

The German sub-lieutenant blew his nose and said nothing, looking at the deck. The translator looked at Hartenstein.

Hartenstein pulled himself to his full height. "I have much to say." He turned away from the American Captain and faced the civilian witnesses, his eyes settling on the proprietor of the Sign of the Lamb tavern.

"Who is this man Madison and what has he done for your country? He has led you into an unwanted war ... an unnecessary war where a lot of good American people are dying. An unnecessary war because England has changed its rules and now allows you to trade with Europe. Madison knew that, yet, he went ahead with this war, egged on by the hawks in your so-called democratic congress." His voice raised half an octave, punctuating what he said with his finger. "You have been duped. Democracy does not exist. You send your representatives to Washington to express your collective views and they soon return selling Washington's views to you ... hence, this war."

Matthew noticed that a few of the civilians were beginning to nod, agreeing with Hartenstein.

"Your militia are weak and badly disciplined. The sole reason for this is they elect their own officers. There is no officer class, people who know military strategy. America lost at Queenston because your militia disobeyed their officers. These officers wouldn't do anything about it because they are elected and want to be elected again."

Hartenstein turned and pointed at the American Captain, who sat stern faced behind his desk, his mouth working like he was having a hard time swallowing.

"The *Chesapeake* is not a democracy and it is a strong fighting vessel. The *Constitution* is not a democracy and look at the glory she brings to the United States. Democracy weakens all it touches. It weakens armies. It weakens countries. The United States should be able to walk into Canada but is too weak and disorganized to do it. What the United States needs is a good solid government run by people who earn the right to be there through their deeds, and not by the number of votes they can purchase. A disciplined people have a sense of country and a view to the future. What kind of country will your children inherit—"

The proprietor of the Sign of the Lamb tavern couldn't take it any longer. He jumped to his feet and held his fist toward Hartenstein. "I'll tell you the kind of country our children will inherit," he yelled, his face was hot with anger. He ignored the American Captain who was pounding his desk with a gavel.

"They will inherit a country that will allow them to grow to the maximum of their talent and need. A country where they are free to think and say what they believe, verbally or in writing. They will inherit a country where they are free to travel and live anywhere within its borders, and where every person is treated equally under the law. Politicians will always be politicians. In this country we can at least kick them out after four years."

The proprietor turned to face the American Captain and pointed at Hartenstein. "In his United States there would be one superior race, a pure German race. All other races would be sub-cultures whose only opportunity in life would be to serve their superiors. There would be no democracy. The country's leaders would be those who could persuade enough people to support their view and seize the government by force. He serves as an example as to what the country would be like. He proclaimed himself Fuehrer. If anyone disagreed with him, he was executed. As the evidence showed, he nailed my good friend, a man known to most of you ... he nailed Ulrich into a barrel and sent him over Niagara Falls. It was he who ... who ... oh, the hell with it!"

The proprietor's anger got the better of him. He rushed at Hartenstein, gripped him around the neck and began to squeeze. The American Captain banged his gavel and yelled for the guards. The proprietor and Hartenstein fell to the deck, Hartenstein struggling to free himself, his tongue protruding from the force of the choke. The proprietor was a strong man and it took three burly sailors to pry his hands loose, pull him away from Hartenstein, and restrain him.

Hartenstein gasped for air, vomiting onto the canvas deck covering. He slowly stood to his feet, recovering enough to straighten his tunic.

"Enough!" The American Captain was visibly angry. He banged his gavel. "Lieutenant Hartenstein. It is the judgment of this court that you shall be taken from this cabin and locked in the bilboes until six bells of the forenoon watch. At that time, you will be hung by the neck, until you are dead, from the main course yardarm. May God rest your soul. I doubt it!"

"Sub-Lieutenant Godt. Your defence of following orders is no defence. Some orders should not be obeyed. Sometimes it's a high cost that decency extracts, but God is your final judge. However, I'm prepared to be lenient. It is the judgment of this court that you be taken from this cabin and locked in the bilboes until six bells of the forenoon watch. At that time, you will witness the death of your commander. Then, a firing squad will be assembled and, in honourable fashion … you will be shot. May God rest your soul."

He banged his gavel. "This court is adjourned."

As official witnesses to the executions, Matthew and Bell were guests overnight at the Sign of the Lamb tavern. The morning dawned grey and snowing, big flakes that were heavy with water, the type children love. On board the *Chesapeake*, Matthew looked toward the town of Boston which was invisible behind the white, softly falling curtain. The snow wasn't sticking, the wet flakes melted as soon as they hit the holystoned boards of the quarterdeck. The good people of Boston materialized, without noise, from the invisible into the visible, to gather at the end of Long Wharf alongside the *Chesapeake*. There was still over two hours to go and the crowd was so large that the people at the back were only light grey shadows.

Matthew studied the crowd and was amazed at what he saw. Whole families had gathered, many brought their breakfast with them, mothers distributed bread and cheese to children bundled against the snow. Matthew couldn't rid himself of a sick feeling in his stomach at the thought of witnessing executions. Why are all these people here?

He looked to the main course yardarm where a crew were busy rigging the halter. On the quarterdeck to seaward, a crew was loading a cannon with powder and wadding only. On the quarterdeck a grating was being rigged. The sub-lieutenant will be lashed to the grating to face the firing squad.

"Why would all these people want to be here, Yeoman?" Matthew saw that Bell was looking pale and wondered if he was hung over after last night at the tavern where the proprietor was free with his rum. It was probably the thought of witnessing executions and Matthew wondered if he looked the same.

"I asked that question of myself, Bell. I think there is something about an execution … about witnessing someone's death that fascinates a macabre side of human nature. Perhaps people wonder how they would react if it was their neck that was feeling the noose." Matthew had thought the same things himself. What would it be like knowing that he had only an hour to live? Then thirty minutes … a minute? The last breath, the last heartbeat, the last thought! Would he want to get it over with? Would he struggle and yell his head off? Does your mind take over? He'd heard that victims of execution can seem very calm, perhaps the calm of having a knowledge that eludes most men, that being the knowledge of when they are going to die.

At 1045 hours, Matthew and Bell were told to join the official witnesses who gathered along the quarterdeck's starboard side, their backs to the crowd. Below them, the good citizens of Boston were jostling for position, using elbows to move others aside. Matthew looked to seaward where a good many cutters and whalers backed water, boats from vessels within the anchorage, all loaded with eager spectators. The ship's company lined the forecastle rail and both gangways. The gun crew was in position with the cannon run out. Marines were smartly drawn up in two ranks along the railing at the break of the quarterdeck forward of the main mast. The ship's drummer boy was standing—waiting.

The snow had let up, changing to a light rain when the American Captain emerged from the companionway that led to his cabin. It must be time. Matthew felt his bowels turning fluid and he needed to visit the head. He just wished to hell he didn't have to be here.

"Bring up the prisoners." The American Captain looked elegant in his full dress uniform, his features intense.

A boson's mate ran down the companionway stairs to the gun deck, his pipe sounding "still," yelling, "Do yah hear?"

The German sub-lieutenant was brought to the quarterdeck, escorted by a guard each side, holding him by his arms which were tied behind his back. He looked very pale; a small twitch persisted in the left corner of his mouth. He was making a game attempt at showing no fear but his eyes were flicking from side to side, betraying anxiety. His breath escaped his body in small clouds of steam as he was led to the grating and turned to face forward with his back to it. Lines were passed through the grating and around his body and tied tightly. One was around his upper chest under his arms, another around his waist; two more lines secured his legs. He was fastened in such a way that when he was dead and limp, his body would remain erect, only his head would fall forward. The deck shook as eight United States Navy sailors, boots on their feet, were marched in single file to form a line twenty feet in front of him, muskets on their shoulders. At first, Matthew wondered why they didn't face their victim but were turned to face forward. Then he remembered that the sub-lieutenant was to watch the hanging of Hartenstein.

Looking back at the sub-lieutenant he noticed that the man seemed calm, his eyes were closed and his face turned up into the rain. Matthew felt that he was looking at a man who, after a long absence, had discovered that he was finally going home.

CHAPTER 30

▼

Lieutenant Hartenstein, Fuehrer of the National Socialist Party of America, tripped on the top step of the companionway and had to be kept from falling by a guard who grabbed his arm. He stopped for a moment and looked toward the sub-lieutenant. His guards pushed him, urging him to move. He twisted from their grasp and began walking directly for the gangway, leaving the guards looking confused. There was no sentry at the gangway and he actually began to descend to the wharf, the people at the bottom starting to move aside to let him pass.

Matthew started to move but the American Captain beat him to it, hurriedly grabbing Hartenstein by the collar and hauling him back on deck. Hartenstein was unable to keep his balance and fell with his back to the deck. Matthew saw the man shrug and smile at the American Captain. Matthew had to admire the man. He had tried, and he had failed. His strategy had worked with the Mohawks at Queenston. The conversation of the crowd grew more excited for they were getting their entertainment.

The American Captain hauled Hartenstein to his feet and with the ease of a ballet dancer, spun the man around to face his executioner. The hangman looked away to avoid Hartenstein's eyes, seeming to take an interest in the men lined up to tail the rope that would haul Hartenstein to the end of the yardarm.

Hartenstein stiffened, squared his shoulders, and strode toward the hangman. Then, just as quickly, he made a right turn to the rail, and began speaking loudly in German. The translator was there for the purpose of translating the prisoner's last words.

"Before this hour is over, I, Klaus Hartenstein will be executed, dead and buried. You will say that I have descended into Hell to sit with the Devil. You simpletons may not understand this but one hundred years from now, I will rise again from the dead! I will sit with my Fuehrer, Adolph Hitler, destined overlord of Europe, Great Britain, Canada, Russia, and yes, these United States. Your descendants will serve the Aryan—"

"Shut up—you arn't no Messiah!" The American Captain forcefully pulled Hartenstein away from the rail and thrust him toward the hangman. The two guards held him tightly. The hangman went to tighten a leather strap around Hartenstein's ankles.

"Belay that," the American Captain bellowed. He put his face close to Hartenstein's. "I want to see this bastard dance. You are lucky that I don't have the knot placed under your chin. Your parade is over … time now for you to pay the jesters."

The hangman dropped the belt, grabbed the noose, and slipped it over Hartenstein's head, leaving it to hang loose around his neck. The two guards turned him to face the American Captain who pulled folded pages from his tunic where he'd kept them from the rain. He unfolded them and began to read.

"Klaus Hartenstein, it is the judgment of the American people that you are guilty of the crimes of murder, unlawful assembly, forming an illegal militia, kidnapping, unlawful confinement, trespassing, and a general disregard for the United States, its peoples, its government, and its constitutional guarantees. You are now to pay the price for these outrageous crimes. May God rest your soul." He folded the papers. "Prepare the prisoner!"

Hartenstein looked like he was about to say something when the hangman pulled his noose tight, cutting off his ability to speak, the knot with its thirteen turns biting into the muscle below his left ear. The two guards lifted Hartenstein bodily to the top of the gunwale where he almost lost his balance.

"Oops! You arn't going ta swindle the hangman that easily," said the guard who steadied Hartenstein on the gunwale.

The drummer boy began beating a steady rhythm, the sailors tailing the rope tensed, ready to dash on command. The gunner tightened his lanyard, his head turned towards his captain.

Matthew couldn't take his eyes off Hartenstein. He found he was fascinated.

"Sting the bastard up!"

The sailors began running with the line, jerking Hartenstein into the air, the noose biting into his neck jerking his head to the right as the weight of his body took full effect.

The cannon fired to seaward causing Matthew to jump. He looked toward the cannon; his heart pounding, but his eye caught something else. When the cannon went off, he saw the sailor at the front of the executioner's line fall to the deck, a neat hole in the left side of his head, the right side of his head disappeared into a pink mist. A gusher of blood spurted a foot into the air, falling off as the body's blood pressure subsided. The following sailors, unprepared, tripped and fell over the body, letting go of the line. Hartenstein, who was ascending toward the main course spar with his feet kicking, his face purple and his tongue protruding, plunged to the wharf. Matthew ran to the rail and saw that Hartenstein had landed on an overly large woman who cushioned his fall.

A group of men, Matthew recognized them as the U-boat's sailors, grabbed Hartenstein and began dragging him in the direction of the U-boat. One of them was desperately trying to loosen the noose but was having trouble. Hartenstein was still choking to death, flailing his feet, and kicking those trying to help him, his eyes open and protruding. The man took a knife and cut the noose from the rope leading to the yardarm, then working quickly, turned Hartenstein over so he could place his knife on the back of the noose, and began sawing. The line parted, lay by lay.

"Shoot him! Shoot the bastard!" The American Captain was furious, pushing subordinates and onboard witnesses out of his way as he followed the action on the dock. The only sailors who had muskets were the firing squad. They ran toward the forecastle, the sailors on the starboard gangway hastily moved out of their way. Matthew followed.

"We can't shoot!" The sailor looked pained as he spoke, his voice pleading. "We'll kill some innocent people!"

The American Captain didn't answer. He drew his sword, climbed to the gunwale, and leapt into the crowd.

"Make way! For the love of God … make way for me!" He tried pushing his way along, holding his sword high so as not to injure the men, women, and children who were scrambling to get out of his path.

The press of the crowd was no handicap to Hartenstein's men. They formed a wedge and punched and kicked anyone in their way. A young boy screamed as he was pushed off the wharf. He hung by his fingers to save himself, only to be crushed by the moving hull of the *Chesapeake*. His remains slipped down a piling and into the harbour. The water rippled around his squashed, floating body as small fish began to feed.

All these things, Matthew saw. He made his way through the press of sailors to the rail at the beakhead bulkhead just as a musket fired. The ball ripped apart the shoulder of a German sailor as he ran down the gangway of the U-boat. The American sentry threw away his musket and turned to run, nowhere to go except the sea. He was grabbed from behind by the hair and his head pulled back, his scream was cut short by the knife that slashed his throat. The blood from his main arteries turned to froth from the air escaping his lungs. His body was callously discarded over the side of the gangway. The U-boat crew was back in possession of their vessel, the German sailors disappearing through the conning tower hatch. Their captain was still on the wharf being dragged toward his command.

Two of the U-boat crew descended to the wrought iron deck where the 20 mm anti-aircraft cannon was mounted. The magazine was still loaded, the Americans didn't have the technical knowledge to remove it, and they didn't even know it could be removed. One sailor cocked the weapon, tucked his shoulder into the weapons rest and swung the barrel to point at the bowsprit of the *Chesapeake*.

On seeing this, Matthew shouted a warning—a warning that went unheeded for American sailors were swarming over the beakhead bulkhead and onto the head gratings. One American sailor, with a coil of line over his shoulder, ran out along the bowsprit after crossing the grating style gangway from the forecastle. Below him, the German pulled the trigger.

Armour piercing shells ripped into the bowsprit. Every fifth shell was a tracer that left a curl of smoke in its path. Splinters flew from the flying jib boom, a bobstay parted, a deadeye securing the topmast preventer stay flew into minuscule fragments. One bullet took off the running American's foot, causing the man to sit down hard, the jib boom grinding into his crotch. He sat there momentarily, intense pain etching his features until he was ripped apart by shells. His upper half tumbled in a grotesque dive to the U-boats deck. His lower half remained straddling the jib boom, his intestines uncoiling to hang vertically from his torso, a grotesque rope that dripped blood and rainwater.

The German swung the machine cannon toward the sailors gathered on the head gratings. It was a slaughter. Shells thrashed into the waiting sailors, blood and body parts falling through the gratings, and onto the U-boat's deck or into the water. A sailor, descending a line to the head grating, had his head exploded by a shell. As a row of holes stitched its way toward the forecastle deck, the assembled Americans began to fall back in panic.

Terror gripped the mass of good Boston people on the wharf—a need to flee the death that was spitting from the barrel of the "musket from Hell." Those who had the misfortune to fall were trampled. Mothers, attempting to shield their fallen children, died along with their offspring.

The anti-aircraft gun swung toward the fleeing Bostonians but it didn't fire. The magazine was empty, the breechblock stayed open.

Matthew could see the American Captain pinned against a warehouse wall by the force of the fleeing crowd, struggling to free himself, his sword held above his head.

Looking forward, he saw that the U-boat had slipped its lines and a lone German sailor stood on the conning tower bridge. The sky opened, the rain increased in volume ten fold, the U-boat disappeared from view, masked by the downpour. On the wharf the American Captain, a vague shadow, leaned against a large crate. The rain bounced off the deck forming a mist. Forward on the head gratings and bowsprit, bodies, pieces of bodies, and the gratings themselves, were purged clean of blood by the rain. A light pink wash dripped to the cheeks of the head to form small rivers around the hawse holes and down the main wale.

The rain eased slightly. Matthew could see the U-boat heading toward the harbour entrance. In the rain haze its low silhouette reminded him of a basking shark waiting to pounce on an unsuspecting quarry. The people of the town of Boston, and the families of the Germans that Hartenstein recruited into his sordid militia, had been its prey. Many lives had been lost, happy families decimated, and property destroyed.

Matthew felt a sense of failure for he had let down the Old Man. He'd been charged with the responsibility of containing or destroying the U-boat and it had gotten away from him. Somehow, in all the excitement of the last few days, he had fogotten about the U-boat's crew. Matthew cuffed the rain from his eyes and looked at the grating where the sub-lieutenant had been trussed to await the firing squad. Where he'd gone, or when or how he'd gotten away, he had no fugging idea.

CHAPTER 31

▼

Matthew's childhood fantasies were filled with adventure, glory, brave deeds, and swashbuckling heroes. Of course, with age came reason—a coming to terms with actualities. Adventure, a word easily spoken, usually meant a risking of life and limb for uncertain goals. Now he knew, as he stood on the deck of *HBMS Shannon* watching the approach of the *Chesapeake*, that he was facing reality. Some childhood fantasies should never come true. He really did not want to be there.

He looked across the water toward *Blackfoot* where the Old Man was maintaining the English Captain's dictated distance from the upcoming battle. He would much sooner be over there, an observer rather than a participant. He never volunteered to be here, and neither had Ordinary Seaman Bell who was staring at the approaching *Chesapeake*. Their job was to get the communications gear, that wasn't used for the trip to Niagara, together for return to *Blackfoot*. They were isolated by circumstance—the approach of the *Chesapeake* curtailed their operation. He and Bell were left to face the horrors of a historic naval battle, wooden ship against wooden ship. Matthew was feeling alone and very vulnerable.

The *Shannon* had the best-trained gun crews in the Royal Navy. While the Admiralty were sticklers for spit and polish, it being more important that the cannon be properly blackened than properly handled, the English Captain was a fanatic for gun drill, incurring the Admiralty's wrath for wasting powder. The Admiralty's preference had been shown to place good British lives and stout British ships in jeopardy, with the loss of many ships of war to the fledgling American navy. The English Captain's philosophy was about to be put to the test.

Matthew and Bell were ordered leave the gangway for the better-protected gun deck where they were met by Newlove, newly promoted gun captain of an eighteen-pound cannon.

"Here," said Newlove, handing Matthew and Bell dark blue bandannas. "You better put these over your ears or you'll be deaf after the first broadside."

"I may be dead after the first broadside," said Bell as he took the bandanna. Newlove smiled and gave Bell a friendly punch in the shoulder.

"It is possible. It's something you'll learn not to ponder. If you've got to pray, pray now." Newlove used his bare foot to spread some sand to an area missed by the sailor with the pail of sand, then returned to his gun.

"I didn't think what I said was funny, Yeo," said Bell, his voice quivering.

A boson's mate ran down the companionway ladder from the quarterdeck sounding "still" on his pipe. The steady note was shrill, its ear piercing sound captured by the confines of the gun deck. *Shannon's* crew stood silently beside their charges.

"Cast loose your guns." The order was given by the first lieutenant and repeated by the lieutenant in charge of the battery.

Matthew and Bell moved out of the way as Newlove and his crew swung into action, their feet kicking up dust from the sanded deck. The orders came in quick succession, barely allowing the crew time to carry out each routine.

"Level your guns."

Matthew looked along the battery, impressed by the precision of the gun crews, much like a drill team on parade.

"Tompions—load with cartridge."

The waiting powder monkey held forward his leather cylinder from which was drawn the cloth, powder-filled cartridge. The sea had already hardened the boy who couldn't be more than twelve years old. He gave Matthew a passing glance, turned, and trotted off toward the ladder that led to the decks below, and the hanging powder room.

"Home," said Newlove, announcing contact between his priming wire and the cartridge.

"Shot your guns."

A wad, followed by a round shot, were shoved into the barrel, and driven hard onto the cartridge.

"Run out your guns."

Overhead lanyards were pulled and the gun port opened admitting daylight and cool air that assailed the sweating bodies of the crew. The crew heaved on tackles and the ponderous cannon slowly rolled, carriage wheels squealing, until the muzzle was outboard of the port's sill. The cannon was now ready for priming.

The crew stood back from the gun as Newlove peered along the barrel. The *Chesapeake* was visible, approaching bow on, still at a considerable distance. Matthew was apprehensive. When was the last time he had said a prayer and really meant it? It wasn't at church parade, where the focus was on ceremony rather than your inner spirit. For most sailors, church parade was a time to catch up on sleep. If he said a prayer now, would he be hypocritical? Does God accept a hypocrite into heaven? If he did pray, he would pray that today wasn't the day he would find out!

"Prime your guns." The order startled Matthew from his thoughts.

Newlove shoved his priming wire down the cannon's vent and pierced the cloth cartridge, making a hole exposing the powder. He then filled the vent and pan with priming powder from his powder horn. He checked his flint, pulled back the hammer, and assumed his aiming position, crouched behind the cannon beyond its length of recoil. The bow of the *Chesapeake* filled the port. Matthew placed his hands over his ears.

"Fire!"

Newlove pulled his lanyard. The breech of the cannon was wreathed by powder smoke from the pan and vent before the cannon itself fired, belching smoke and flame. The noise was extreme and the reaction violent. The cannon recoiled to the ends of its tackles, lifting the carriage a good inch off the deck and putting great strain on the tackles, timbers, and knees.

When the broadside was fired, all cannons recoiling simultaneously, the strain on the *Shannon* was excessive, even though she was a well-found ship. The noise was excruciating, causing great agony. Matthew's head was ringing; his eardrums stretched in spite of the fact that he remembered to cover his ears, which were already covered by the bandanna, and open his mouth to relieve pressure. The flame was consumptive, robbing the air of oxygen, the smoke all encompassing, causing Matthew's eyes to smart, his nose to run, and his throat to scratch. He began to cough uncontrollably; a twinge of pain accompanied each breath drawn.

Bell was on his knees bringing up a large amount of phlegm.

The gun was being serviced the second it came to a stop. The worm was driven down the barrel to remove any burning particles of flannel cartridge. It was followed by a wet sponge which extinguished what the worm left behind. The loading procedure began again only this time; each gun crew was on its own, working their gun at their own speed—their fastest possible speed!

The *Shannon* shook to her floor timbers as the *Chesapeake* drove into her side. She heeled to port with the impact. Beyond the muzzle of Newlove's cannon, Matthew caught a glimpse of an enemy gun port, the muzzle of its cannon a black circle through which could be seen—eternity. In the suspended seconds before it spit fire, smoke and iron, Matthew heard Newlove say a time worn naval prayer.

"For what we're about to receive, may the Lord make us—" The gun port filled with smoke and flame, the right side timber exploded into jagged wooden fragments. Matthew was aware of only fractions of images, all nightmarish, and all in slow time. A man's arm cart-wheeled through the air, bright red blood from the severed end left a decorative pattern on the deck head timbers. The scar on the side of the cannon barrel where the ball glanced off before it took the powder monkey in the chest, leaving his young body a mass of jellied flesh. The cannon slued sideways, knocking those that served her to the deck, crushing limbs, abdominal cavities and chests. A man's head was pinned to the gun port's left side timber by the cannon's barrel, bursting it as a sledge hammer would a cocoa nut. His eyes focused on a sharp splinter of oak as it pin-wheeled directly toward him.

Matthew saw the Devil's lair, felt the Devil's hot breath singe his exposed skin. He felt the Devil's probing, claw-tipped fingers, tear at his uniform seeking access to his vital organs. He looked the Devil in the eye and wasn't afraid. The splinter tore along his ribs, tearing apart his number five jacket, bruising his flesh. Out of the corner of his eye he saw Bell, who had moved behind him, lurch backward and fall to the deck.

In the midst of battle where action and reaction happen in split second intervals, it would be impossible to put a time or situation to the change from civility to crudity. The need for restraint and decorum gives way to a blood-lust, a fierce, destructive reaction driven by the need to protect or survive. Something in the mind snaps, a weapon is selected, and the enemy is targeted.

Matthew's inner demon was awake; all its energy concentrated in Matthew's chest, his diaphragm compressed his lungs. His mouth opened, the pressure released as a blood thirsty, chilling, primal scream. Groups of muscles tensed, storing energy for instant release. His breath felt hot, his field of vision became narrow and sharply focused, and the periphery became a black curtain. His soul had left his body to be replaced by another more archaic in thought, more extreme in action, and more selfish in motive—a being that valued only its life. Matthew looked through its bloodshot eyes, breathed through its foul mouth, and killed using its practiced skill.

He became one of a great number, a wave of yelling, cutting, thrusting tars that leapt through the gun port and across the gap between the two grinding vessels to meet the American defenders on the *Chesapeake's* gun deck.

Flashes of small arms fire pierced the smoke haze that obscured the enemy. A ragged volley staggered the attackers, many falling face first to the deck, their whoops and cries of encouragement turning to guttural laments. The press from behind, as more British tars crowded onto the gun deck, forced those in front to carry the attack forward.

The fight became personal, focused within the perimeter of a private struggle, hand to hand, life or death. Matthew forgot his mates, his lifetime experience, the war, and even the year. His mind concentrated his body's vigour, substance, and intuition into one powerful package with one objective—to overwhelm.

He saw their faces but didn't catalogue them as human. He saw their weapons but didn't register the threat. He felt their blows yet experienced no discomfort. He heard their vexations; saw their anger, surprise, and pain. He saw their deaths. He felt detached from the act of killing.

He butted, bit, punched, scratched and gouged. He screamed in his enemy's ears. He damned their persons, their heritage, insulted their intelligence, and criticized their abilities. He disfigured, maimed, disembowelled, and decapitated.

A face moved though Matthew's line of vision, only to return again, contorted with anger. The bellow that assaulted Matthew's ears was matched by his own, a howl that originated in the caves of the Neanderthal, echoing through the millennium, voiced by millions of sailors and soldiers engaged in deadly combat on scarred decks or muddy battlefields.

Matthew's opponent was immense. The momentum of his attack drove him backward, his pursuer pushing other combatants out of the way as minor annoyance, forcing him against the breach of a cannon. The man towered over him, a mountain of bunched muscle, a palisade of humanity that seemed impregnable. A colossal arm slowly raised the red stained blade of a cutlass in a high arc.

Matthew's demon spoke for the first time; it's voice echoing through the tunnel of ages. "I know you. It's been … centuries!"

The man's eyes opened wide, the pupils rafting in an inflamed sea, and focusing on the top of Matthew's head. The man's mouth contorted with effort, bunching his total energy into this one blow. "Hiel … Hartenstein!" The cutlass began its death stroke.

Matthew crouched, collecting his power in his legs, his cutlass gripped in both hands, and aimed at his assailant's unprotected stomach. He launched his body upward, a piston driving against the momentum of attack. His mind momentarily comprehended the shout, the motivation of his attacker's fury. His cutlass entered the man's abdomen below the navel and was driven upward though the intestines, liver, stomach, and lungs before glancing along the back rib cage.

The man's momentum carried him onto Matthew. His plunging cutlass struck the cannon's barrel and shattered. Matthew's cutlass was wrenched from his hand, his other hand and arm instinctively trying to fend off the collapsing man. The weight was too much for him and an avalanche of quivering humanity buried him. He felt the man's hand moving between them, reaching toward his neck. Strong fingers gripped the edge of his windpipe and began digging, seeking to work their way into his flesh. He fought for breath.

The desire for life, for self-preservation, often results in the joining together of opposites into a single force. The demon of the underworld that was the agglomeration of all warriors' tortured, twisted aggression, and the soul that is Matthew, who personified the civilized, decent, modern person, joined together. They were allies in the same cause. Their combined strengths were mustered, focused, and utilized. His soul followed the directions of his demon. Their merged cries were loud and furious in Matthew's brain. The dying man's fingers remained locked on his windpipe, the pressure increased as the tendons contracted in spasmodic convulsion. More help was needed! More help was summoned! More help arrived!

The strength of a thousand sailors, a gathering of sailor's souls, special duty men from wars present and past; all mustered within Matthew's body and took up their action stations. Their voices combined in a shout that emanated from the bowels of Hell.

CHAPTER 32

▼

The American Captain lay dead on *Chesapeake's* orlop deck, his final words to his men, "Don't give up the ship," went unheeded. The battle was over; the flag of the United States Navy was lowered. The *Chesapeake* had struck her colours.

Along the decks of the *Shannon* and the *Chesapeake*, British and American sailors lowered their weapons; most men fell silent, their bodies flooding with relief, surprised to be alive, checking themselves for wounds.

After the battle came the trauma, both individual and personal. Joyous reunions between friends who hugged each other, laughing in spontaneous celebration; the search, the prolonged suspense, anticipation of happiness, dread of discovery, disappointment or loss; sad findings, expressions of grief at the death of a mate; involuntary gestures of affection, closing a dead friends eyes, straightening his body and tidying his clothing; recoil, stomach contracting, up-chucking revulsion, the initial reaction to the mangled mess that was your friend; hopeful apprehension, comforting words of encouragement, a search for help, assistance, any aid that may be available for a wounded mess mate.

The Jimmy found Bell alive and wandering the gun deck of the *Shannon*, babbling to himself, his uniform in tatters, a large bruise on his right hip, and his face and hands scorched. He was escorted gently to the upper deck where one of *Blackfoot's* medical assistants tended to him.

Matthew was found by Ordinary Seaman Parsons, his bloody cutlass gripped in his right hand, leaning against a gun carriage talking to Newlove, and staring at the body of a giant man whose intestines lay splayed outside his abdominal cavity. They were discussing the man, who he was, and where they'd seen him before. Matthew was wheezing with each breath as he spoke, his throat hurt like hell, he suspected it was badly bruised. His uniform was almost torn from his body, the remaining parts stuck to his skin by dried blood and mucus.

"Can you walk, Yeoman?"

Matthew looked up, surprised to see Parsons. "Yes, I think so." He coughed, grabbing his neck to try and ease the pain caused by speaking. "How is Bell? Have you found him? Is he okay?"

Upon his return to *Blackfoot*, Matthew was cleaned up and given a good going-over by the surgeon; his bruises were salved and covered by soft cotton bandages. He was told to sleep. He wanted to sleep but his brain kept him awake. A gut wrenching emotional trauma gripped his body, making him feel as if he was drained of his soul. He couldn't turn off the cacophony of battle; the screams, curses, and laments of friends and victims; the eardrum splitting explosions of cannon and pistol. He couldn't turn off his personal projector that repeated over and over the same scenes in his mind; the contorted, angry faces of attackers, the surprised, tortured faces of his victims. His fight for body and soul, just trying to survive, and the surprise of having survived—shouldn't he be celebrating? He should hate the vanquished, or perhaps he should have sympathy for them. Why did he survive? Please God, just make his brain shut up. He lay in his sick bay berth and stared at the pipes and electrical wires that ran along the deckhead, and sweated.

When action stations sounded, he ignored the advice of the surgeon, and slowly made his way to the bridge. Anything, even more action would help, he just had to quiet his mind. Upon arriving he found that the Jimmy had spotted the U-boat's periscope and *Blackfoot* was manoeuvring to attack. The echo of the U-boat's signature on the ASDIC's bridge repeater pierced the evening gloom.

"That bastard! That God damned bastard!" The Old Man stared over the bridge screen, and then moved to the voice pipes.

"Bridge … ASDIC." He paused to listen for the reply. "Give me the compass bearing of the U-boat."

Matthew looked to where the *Shannon* and the *Chesapeake* were outlined against the crimson sunset.

Shannon was shaking out her sails, men could be seen out along her yards. A large cable had been passed to the *Chesapeake* in preparation for towing. The scene, stark against the setting sun, had a peaceful look to it. Hard to believe that just a few hours ago the two vessels were locked together in mortal conflict.

Beyond the two vessels a flotilla of small boats was returning to Boston, the audience was filing out of the coliseum. The American gladiator had battled the

English lion and the lion had won. Hadn't those people had enough of maiming and killing? Did they need a naval battle to provide further entertainment? Matthew looked at the clear sky. He looked at Jupiter, the brightest planet after Venus. How did it go—a boat, a sail, and a star to steer by—something like that? The three quarter moon would be rising soon. How did he remember that? He breathed deep, feeling the oxygen surge to his extremities. Yes! Yes! Yes! It's good to be alive! He survived! He survived!

Matthew looked to the eastern horizon. A line of fog, a black arch that cut off the stars, obscured the sky to the east. It was a strange feeling, a magnetic pull, a compulsion; Matthew couldn't take his eyes from it. Behind him the Old Man and the Jimmy were busy lining up the U-boat and Matthew couldn't give a fug.

"Bearing three five five, sir. Doppler indicates target approaching. Range one five oh," reported the HSD.

"Very good … inform the anti-submarine control officer. Steer three five five." *Blackfoot* heeled with the turn.

Matthew was transfixed, the battle was forgotten, and the U-boat was forgotten. Panic was beginning to take root in his bowels. The fog bank grew taller, the top beginning to collapse in on its self. Lightning flashed between its different layers.

"Fire depth charges!"

Matthew was vaguely aware of the coughs made by the beam depth charge throwers. His apprehension was giving way to a feeling of absolute calm. He reached out with both arms as the fog bank embraced *Blackfoot* in a swirling vortex—a mutual gesture of welcome. A gesture one would make to an old friend. One who remembers the old times!

EPILOGUE

▼

"Holy shit ... hard to Starboard!" yelled Commander Forron, also known as the "Old Man," his voice showing panic.

"Hard to starboard," was the calm reply of the coxswain in the wheelhouse below the bridge.

At first the approaching form was soft, its edges dissolved by the cold mist of a black night. It appeared as a pulsing orange glow, no explanation, with no apparent detail. The noise it made was filtered through the mist, sounding hollow, a distant hiss and pop sounding like frying bacon.

Its heat preceded its form. Vapour rose from the warming surfaces of *HMCS Blackfoot's* metal plating, causing the immediate surroundings to shimmer due to refraction. It was the warm air condensing on the back of his neck that made Yeoman Matthew Brock shiver.

He squinted at the rapidly approaching apparition, urgently searching for details, his vision impaired by the thickening mist on the bridge. He was able to see a dark stripe that split the orange glow vertically from the water's surface. It was the bow of a ship. He could see the bow wave.

"Sir ... it's a ship on fire!" The Old Man didn't hear him, seemingly mesmerized, his eyes danced with reflected flame.

It was on them in seconds, roaring down the port side at a combined speed of at least forty knots. Matthew felt the hair on his forearm singe but he didn't follow the Old Man's example of ducking behind the bridge screen. He split his arms so he could see through them while shading his eyes from the heat. The next few moments were only snapshots, brief encounters with split second images.

The ship as it passed, piloted by God himself, was on fire from stem to stern, the flames fanned astern as if combed by some hidden force. He moved aside as *Blackfoot's* port bridge wing lookout dashed by, his clothing a mass of flame, his face distorted with fear, and his screams lost in the chaos.

Matthew stared at the burning form of a man on the forward ladder of the fire ship, flames a blow torch from the eye holes of a blackened skull. It was becoming difficult to breathe; the hungry flames were like a giant vacuum, sucking in oxygen from its surroundings.

"She looks old," he said to himself, as he watched her pass. Her design was early twentieth century, easily recognizable by the vertical sheer of the bow that was topped by an overly tall jack staff. A large hawse hole, housing a naval style anchor, was a tornado of flame. Circular deadlights that ran horizontally in two rows along the heavily armored hull, were each an individual blast furnace that shot a column of intense fire perpendicular to the hull, to be swept back by the speed of the vessel's passage. The forecastle deck, which was long and uncluttered, was a mass of sheeted flames that reached astern to play the air currents around two giant turrets, their barrels askew, each spewing dense, blue smoke. On the bridge, the charred skeleton of a man, the ship's captain perhaps, was still standing, bony hands gripping the forward screen, clenched teeth still white in a blackened jaw, flame licking between exposed ribs, consuming what may be left internally. Black eye holes stared ahead, the skeleton perhaps considering his last, fateful command.

The fighting director top, that was charred and twisted, leaned precariously aft over the first of two funnels that still spouted black smoke from coal fires below. Her reciprocal engines were still in operation. It was doubtful that there could be men alive, shoveling coal into the hungry furnaces, working the valves and watching the gauges. The aft turret, its armor red hot, was swinging through the compass, the barrels elevating as a unit.

"Fug … there can't be anyone in there!" The turret swung, the barrels foreshortened. Matthew dropped his arms and spun around to face the Old Man.

"It can't … for fug sake … sir!" He turned back to stare at the two caverns that were the barrels, each trailing ribbons of thick smoke, that were leveled at *Blackfoot's* bridge, that were leveled at him.

"Sir … do something …" His voice broke with the tension. He stared at the smoking barrels, sucking for air, and mentally counting his heartbeats. The barrels remained locked on the bridge. He clenched his fists from fear and frustration. There was nothing to do but wait … and hope.

His hands came to the front of his chest, palms in, fingers hooked like claws. *Blackfoot's* bridge drew even with the stern. The ferocious draught of the sucking flames created mini volcanoes that exuded large pieces of metal. Parts of a once proud ship were being spit out of the fire to fall with a quenching hiss in its wake which was marked by small fires; beacons marking its last miles. Matthew held his breath. Maybe! Just maybe! The turret still rotated, the smoking barrels remained aimed at the bridge—at Matthew. He remained focused on them, a fatal fascination, willing them to fire, or, for the sake of sanity, to let him be.

From the North Atlantic to the battlefields of World War One, Matthew's chase of Hartenstien continues in Sailor Soldier—His Father's Compass

HISTORICAL NOTES

By the time Matthew and *HMCS Blackfoot* joined the escort group, convoy SC42 was off the southern tip of Greenland and slowly regrouping after being battered by strong winds and seas. It was also under attack by fourteen U-boats of the Markgraf group. The fictional U-boat—the U-boat whose commander becomes Matthew's nemesis throughout the story—was part of that group. Convoy SC42 left Sydney, Cape Breton, on August 30th, 1941. The original escort consisted of the River Class Destroyer, *HMCS Skeena*, plus three corvettes, the *Kenogami*, the *Orillia*, and the *Albernie*. The escort group was augmented by the addition of two corvettes, *Moose Jaw* and *Chambly*, that were part of a training group out of Halifax. The fictional destroyer, *HMCS Blackfoot*, was part of that training group. Convoy SC42 arrived in Liverpool on September 15th, after having lost sixteen vessels to U-boats.

When Matthew first encountered Robert Fulton's steamboat, *Clermont*, it was heading down the Hudson River on its regular service between New York and Albany. *Clermont* was launched in New York City on August 18, 1807. On her first trip up river to Albany, she paddled the 150 miles at an average of five knots, covering the distance in 33 hours. That September, the *Clermont* began regular service between the two cities, only stopping because of winter ice. Although in this novel greed and ambition caused her destruction, her actual fate is unknown. Robert Fulton's diving boat and torpedo system was designed as described. He first demonstrated his diving boat to Napoleon's navy but they rejected his idea. He then approached the British navy, even destroying a derelict warship with a torpedo, but they rejected it as inhumane. It didn't sit well with the British Admiralty that Fulton first approached Napoleon's navy with his diving boat design. In their opinion, Robert Fulton was a man that would deal with the Devil if he could make a profit. This novel portrays Fulton from the British point of view.

The events that Matthew observed during the battle for Queenston Heights took place much as described in the novel. Major General Isaac Brock, later to be knighted for his leadership, was killed by a Kentucky rifleman when he was leading a second charge up the heights. The route Matthew uses to lead his small force up the bluff and into the trees is actually the one used later by General Roger H. Sheaffe, who joined with the Indians to defeat the Americans on the escarpment.

When Matthew first sighted the British frigate, *Shannon*, and the American frigate, *Chesapeake*, the two vessels were involved in a classic broadside versus broadside battle that is fictional. The only battle between these two frigates took place on June 1, 1813. Captain Lawrence had just taken command of the *Chesapeake* and his crew was new and largely untried. Captain Broke had been in command of the *Shannon* for seven years and his crew was well trained. He was chastised by the Admiralty for wasting powder and balls on training—cannons were to be polished, not shot. The letter that Captain Broke had written never reached Captain Lawrence. He had decided to sail forth and meet the *Chesapeake* which had been sailing off Boston harbour. It was a decision that he would have regretted if he had lived. The battle between these two vessels only lasted fifteen minutes. The Americans were routed; Captain Lawrence was mortally wounded. While being taken below, he said the famous line that became the rallying cry of the American Navy, "Don't give up the ship!" In this novel, the battle is fought at an earlier date to allow for continuity of plot.

GLOSSARY OF NAVAL TERMS

A'cock bill	Anchor hanging and ready to drop
Aldis	A hand held signal lamp
Avast	Stop
All standing	Sleep without getting undressed or come to a sudden halt
Defaulters	Men under punishment
Dhobey	To do your laundry
Eyes of a ship	Foreward end of the bow
Cam ship	Cargo ship with an aircraft mounted on a catapult
Catch a crab	Cause noise or visible splash while rowing
Guns	Gunnery Officer
Gunner (T)	Torpedo Gunnery Officer
Head	Toilet
HF/DF	High Frequency Direction Finder
HSD	Higher Submarine Detection Petty Officer
Irish Pennant	A loose thread on a uniform or a line hanging loose in the rigging
Jimmy	Executive Officer
Killick	Leading Seaman

Kip	Sleep
Kye	Naval hot chocolate
Matlot	French for "sailor"
Number One	Executive Officer
OD	Ordinary seaman
Old Man	Captain
Pusser	Government Issue
SOE	Senior Officer Escorts
Tiddley	Neat and tidy.
Tiddley pink	To have washed or showered
TS	Radio room (Telegraphy Station)
WUPS	Work Up Program for new vessels
Yeoman	Senior signal trade rating on board ship
XO	Executive Officer

978-0-595-45037-4
0-595-45037-7

Printed in the United States
200073BV00009B/117/A